Nora's heart was breaking for little Kaaren and her shattered family.

Sometime later, in the middle of the darkest night, Nora awoke to the sniffling and tears of Kaaren, crying for her mother. Nora gathered the sobbing child into her arms. With hands of love, she brushed the straggles of hair from Kaaren's face and wiped away the tears.

"I . . . uh . . . want . . . my . . . ma. Why doesn't she come?"

Nora murmured responses in her own language, wishing she could say the things in her heart to this grieving child. Ingeborge had told her that her mother had gone to be with Jesus. That she was not coming back. But how could such a little one understand that?

Softly, so she would not wake Mary, Nora began to sing. "Jesus loves me. . . ." As the words and love in the song crept into that silent night, she felt the child relax against her shoulder. Jerky, leftover sobs that wracked the small body tore at Nora's heart. . . .

"Heavenly Father, comfort this family," she prayed. "Bring back the love they've lost and, if You want me to care for them, please find a way. Amen."

LAURAINE SNELLING is a full-time writer who has several books published, including the popular Golden Filly series for junior high girls. Mrs. Snelling resides with her husband in Martinez, California.

Books by Lauraine Snelling

HEARTSONG PRESENTS

HP10—Song of Laughter

Dakota Dawn

Lauraine Snelling

Heartsong Presents

ISBN 1-55748-400-7

DAKOTA DAWN

PRINTED IN U.S.A.

one

Flat. How could any land so huge be so unendingly flat?

Nora Johanson leaned her forehead against the sooty train window. It seemed as if they had not climbed a hill nor traveled through any woods in the last forty years. "Don't be silly," she chided herself. "You haven't been on this train for forty years, it just feels that way." She glanced over at the corpulent man sprawled in the seat across the aisle. She certainly didn't need to worry about her mutterings waking him—snores fit to wake hibernating bears puffed at his walrus mustache.

Besides, he would not have understood a word she said since he obviously did not speak Norwegian and her few, carefully learned English phrases were not understood by most people she met.

She dug a cloth out of her carpetbag and scrubbed at the window, the dirt reminding her of how desperately she wanted a bath. If only she could have bathed in Minneapolis. But she was down to her last few coins and could afford only a small hunk of bread.

What will you do? What will you do? The question beat in time with the clacking train wheels, ever bearing her west. Farther from her beloved mountains and fjords of Norway but closer to the arms of the man she had promised to marry. At fifteen she

5

had been so sure of their love. Now, she could barely remember him. She scrunched her eyes shut to conjure up a picture of Hans Larson but it was easier to see his handwriting on the letters they had exchanged over the last three years.

She carefully drew off her natural wool, knitted mittens and opened her purse to count the coins that were left. One, two, three, four. *Uff da.* No blessed angel had multiplied them while she dozed. Four pennies—all that was left of the money Hans had sent to her.

Her stomach rumbled.

In the last letter, Hans had said it was plenty. But then he had not counted on the overly long, storm-tossed sea passage. Or the tedious wait with the thousands of other immigrants on Ellis Island in this year of 1910. Or the blizzard that stopped the train for twelve hours.

Her stomach rumbled again. Would they never come to another town?

Nora fought back the tears that seemed to hover like persistent bees at the back of her eyelids. She sent a silent plea upward. *Please, make the town hurry.* Or maybe it was the train that should hurry. Whatever.

She leaned her head against the back of the seat. Visions of home danced through her mind. Home— with her family crowded around the white-clothed kitchen table, laughing, teasing, telling funny stories.

A sob caught in her throat. Her sister Clara had promised to come to the new land too, as soon as

Nora could send her passage money. And her brother John. When she closed her eyes she could see them so clearly. She shut off the memories with a snap. Think only of the better times, she told herself. Remembering her loved ones, all bundled up and waving goodbye at the train station in Oslo, cut too deeply.

She blew her nose and wiped the errant tear away. As Mama had always said, "The good Lord will be with you and guide you when we can't." But right now Nora needed a human hug, one that she could touch and feel, and even hear. She sneaked a peak at the man in the other seat. She certainly could hear him. The train trip had not kept him awake.

She focused her attention again to what was out the window. The snow did not surprise her—it would be weeks yet before spring came to the hills and valleys at home. It was just the unending flat-ness of the land. The only rises were the drifts that piled against the buildings and sometimes stopped the train. Several times, the railroad men had been forced to dig through the drifts so the train could continue. It would have helped if the men had al-lowed her to assist them in digging instead of just looking at her as though the wind had frozen her brain. Her brothers would have tossed her a shovel and dared her to out-dig them.

She caught a sigh as it was escaping her throat. Think about Hans, she ordered herself. Think of what a fine man he is, how wonderful it will be to have a home of your own and milk cows again. Think of his promise to buy some chickens in the spring.

Will there be flowers by the house? she wondered, closing her eyes to see them better. *Roses. I'll have pink ones and red, maybe even a scarlet climber.*

Just before she nodded off, she jerked upright. This time through the window she saw the sinking sun fling banners of orange and red, vermillion and gold across the sky. The heaped high, gray clouds were now burnished to shine and glow like the very gates of heaven. As the fiery red sun slipped below the horizon, the clouds faded to lavender and purple—and back to gray.

One thing this flat land does exceedingly well, Nora thought, *is sunsets.* She had never seen such a display—not even over her beloved mountains in Norway. As she watched, she dared not blink in fear that she might miss a single hue.

"I'm sorry, Miss," the woolen-coated conductor said as he paused at her seat. At least he spoke Norwegian. "But we'll be an hour later than I thought." He dragged out his gold watch and peered at its face. "Somewhere around ten, I expect."

"*Mange takk,* thank you," Nora nodded with her words.

"Surely your young man will check at the station, so he'll know our arrival time."

Nora nodded; she seemed to be doing a lot of that. Why didn't she feel the consolation the man was trying to offer? Was something wrong with her hearing? "I . . . I'm sure he'll—Hans'll be there."

Not true, a little voice inside her whispered. *You're sure he won't be there to meet you.*

Nora forced her lips into a smile and thanked the man again. She kept herself from turning around and watching him as he made his way down the length of the car, swaying with the movement of the train. He had boarded the train in Chicago and was beginning to seem like an old friend. The music of her own language cemented that feeling. She had never dreamed she would be at such a loss for words because she spoke only Norwegian.

She started to take out her dictionary but put it back because the light was so dim. She had not been able to concentrate on learning new words for the last two days anyway. Since the Norwegian woman she had traveled with left the train in Wisconsin, Nora had practiced English with no one.

Seeing her reflection in the darkened window, she smoothed a few stray hairs up and tucked them under the thick, golden braids she wore coronet-style. She shook her head. "You really need to brush and rebraid your hair," she whispered to the woman in the glass. "And take a bath." She used her handkerchief to dab at her tongue and rub off a spot on her cheek.

In the reflection she could also see a portion of the car behind her. Polished wood on the walls and ceiling gleamed in the lamplight; the brown fabric of the padded seats was worn in spots; some of the passengers had drawn their window curtains closed against the cold and dark. Not Nora, though—she hated to close herself in anymore than was necessary. The car had looked comfortable in the beginning but these five days of being cooped up had worn on both her body and spirit.

It seemed like another week had passed before the conductor returned, announcing "Soldall. Next stop, Soldall." He stopped beside her. "You take care of yourself, now." He reached up and swung her bag down for her from the overhead racks. "I've already made sure your trunk will get off when you do. I just hate to see a pretty thing like you. . . ."

Nora could feel her cheeks flame at his compliment. "*Mange takk.* I thank you for all you've done. I . . . I'm. . . ." She lifted her chin. "I'll be just fine."

While the train slowed, Nora searched for lights. Surely everyone in the town had not gone to bed already. But, as the train huffed and screeched to a halt, she saw only two lights off in the distance— only two. There must be more than two houses in town; Hans had said this was a big town.

She pictured his letter and tried to remember how his voice sounded. "It's a large town for the area. We have stores, a hotel, a Norwegian Lutheran church and. . . ."

She shook her head to keep herself awake. After all, it was ten o'clock at night.

A lone gaslight hung above the door to the train station. Nora paused a moment at the head of the steps leading down to the platform. It had started to snow again; tiny hard pellets rattled on the roof of the metal car. The square window of the station glowed like a beacon against the blackness of the outside peppered with whirling snow.

The conductor held out his hand. "Be careful going down these steps, Miss," he said with a ready smile. Even with his muffler, he shivered in a draft of bitter wind. "Don't appear anyone's here to meet you." He looked over his shoulder as if hoping that someone—anyone—would make a liar out of him.

Nora bit her bottom lip and forced her mouth into a smile. "I . . . I'm sure Hans will be here. I'll wait for him in the station." She trembled at the thought of another falsehood. She wasn't sure he would be there at all. In fact, she was terrified to admit the nagging feeling she had that something was not right.

"You better ask Oscar, the stationmaster, to come pick up your trunk. It'll get buried if this keeps up." He motioned to a black square farther up the station platform.

The train whistled, as if impatient for the delay.

"You take care of yourself now." The conductor helped her down the last step. "Get right inside before you freeze." He waved his lantern, picked up the metal stool, then stepped aboard as the wheels of the train squealed back to life. "God bless."

Before she could get her scarf wrapped up over her nose, the pelleted snow stung her cheeks. If this is what March is like in North Dakota, what will January be like?

"Please, God, let Hans come soon," Nora whispered as she peered off to the sides of the station building that seemed to hunker down against the swirling snow. Darkness, so black it reached out for her, sent her skidding across ice-coated planks towards the square of light. "*Uff da*," she muttered as she slipped and slid, barely keeping her feet.

The wind helped her push the station door open, but it swirled her black woolen skirt and tugged at her scarf before it retreated in defeat. She slammed the door shut and leaned against it. Why did she feel like she had just battled and barely won? Her wish had been that Hans would be waiting inside to surprise her. He had liked to do that—surprise her and make her laugh. But, when she stared into the darkened corners of the room, she felt the dream fade and disappear.

The stationmaster certainly did not resemble Hans in any way. Short and thin seemed the best words to describe him, from closely clipped hair, to feet that barely touched the floor when the man sat at his desk. He had not risen to greet her but Nora realized right away it was not because of bad manners. The man listened to the telegraph with both his hands and ears.

Nora nodded back at him, left her satchel by the door, then wandered over to the pot-bellied stove near the station desk. She loosened her scarf and let it drape around her neck. While the room temperature was warmer than outside, the heat from the stove failed to reach the door, or the corners, or the benches lining the center of the room.

His tapping finished, the man gave a little hop to get down from his chair and then he limped forward. "May I help you, Miss?" He reached into a back pocket to retrieve a handkerchief. After blowing and wiping his reddened nose, he peered over his metal-rimmed glasses and, starting at her feet, measured her height with his stare.

Nora felt like the giant troll in one of her sister's stories. "I . . . I'm Nora Johanson, from Norway." His intense gaze caused her to falter. "I . . . I wired ahead. Hans Larson, my betrothed, was to meet me tonight. I'm . . . ah sorry, the . . . ah train was late." Why didn't the man say something? Anything? She unclenched her hands in her mittens and extended them to the warmth of the stove. Right now her cheeks felt like they had been sunburned.

Maybe he had not understood a word she had said. She pointed to her chest and repeated her name, louder.

"You don't have to shout." The little man backed away.

Nora breathed a sigh of relief—he had answered in Norwegian. "Did you receive my wire?" she asked.

He nodded.

"Did you give it to Hans Larson?"

The stationmaster shook his head.

"Did Hans contact you?"

A nod. "Close to a week ago. Said he'd return in a day or so. Too far out in the country for me to deliver it." The man limped back to his desk and shuffled some papers in a wire basket. He pulled one out. "Here it is."

Nora felt something clench around her stomach and twist. Hans didn't even know she was arriving today. How could he have met her? She licked her dry, chapped lips. What would she do now?

"The hotel's right up the street. I can take you

there on my way home." The man returned to the
stove and closed the damper. He set the teakettle to
the back and peered through the isinglass windows
to check the coals. A grunt seemed to express his
approval.

"I . . . ah. . . ." Nora could not force the words past
the lump in her throat.

"Yah?" He paused on his uneven journey to the
coat rack.

"Sir, I have no money for a hotel." Nora felt like
crawling under one of the benches. "The trip took
much longer than we planned, than Hans planned.
Perhaps I can sleep here, until Hans comes, that is.
Maybe he'll come first thing in the morning. I won't
bother anyone and. . . ." Her voice trailed off.

"Oscar."

"What?"

"My name's not Sir, it's Oscar."

"Yah, *mange takk*. Mister Oscar, I. . . ."

He was shaking his head again. "Not Mister Oscar. Oscar Weirholtz. But everyone just calls me
Oscar. You can, too."

"*Mange takk*. I. . . ." Nora could feel the tears
clogging her throat and stinging her eyes. She
clamped her lips shut and looked upwards to ward
off the waterworks. She would not cry!

Oscar stopped buttoning his coat. "No money at
all?"

Nora shook her head. "Four pennies."

"Well that old goat at the hotel won't give a room
to anyone who can't pay in advance." He shook his
head. "And, no, you can't stay here. Against the

rules of the railway. No one can be here without the stationmaster or another employee of the Great Northern Railroad."

Nora now knew how an animal in a trap felt. *Dear God, what will I do?* The prayer slipped past her strangled thoughts in spite of herself.

"I know." Oscar reached for his hat. "I'll take you over to Reverend Moen's house. Mrs. Moen will take you in and she'll know how to contact your young man. You'll like her." He turned down the kerosene lamp, leaned over the glass chimney, and blew out the flame.

"Oh, my trunk." Nora stopped in midstride. "It's still out by the track. I forgot all about it."

Oscar groaned. "Can't it wait . . . no, I suppose not." He struck a match and lit another lantern hanging by the door. When it flared satisfactorily, he set it on the floor and pulled mittens from his pocket. "Come on, then. You'll have to help me. We can probably skid it on the ice, but best be careful." He grabbed the wire handle and, swinging the lantern, stepped outside into the black and cold.

Nora pulled her scarf up over her nose and followed him. When they reached the trunk, he handed her the lantern and grabbed one of the rope handles. "You push."

After they broke it loose from the ice, the trunk slid easily. Nora followed behind until they came to the step and then she set the lantern down and hoisted along with Oscar. The trunk screeched its way over the threshold.

"We can leave it here," Oscar said, nodding toward the wall. "One of the men will bring it down on a wagon in the morning."

"Yah, that will be fine," Nora brushed the snow off the top of the trunk so no moisture would seep inside it. Her quilts, hand-embroidered linens, and household treasures painted with rosemaling designs had not left much room for her clothing. She dusted off the last of the white powder from the trunk and then shook her mittens clean. "*Mange takk*. Thank you very much. I am sorry to be so much trouble."

Oscar nodded, checked the stove and, picking up the lantern, led the way out the door, carefully locking it behind him. "No, here, I'll take that." He held out the lantern in exchange for her heavy bag.

Nora looked down at the small man and hid a smile; she stood nearly a foot taller than he. As he swung off through the stinging snow, the bag bumped against his gimpy leg. She hurried to keep up with him so the lantern could light both their paths.

When they stepped from behind the station, the wind snatched at her scarf and huffed to extinguish the flickering light. Dark buildings lined the street now carpeted with white snow.

Oscar strode down the center of the road. "Less ice this way," he shouted to be heard above the whistling wind. While the falling snow stung all the skin it could find, each gust of wind made the visibility worse.

Nora knew that this storm was a playful kitten compared to the fierce lions of Norwegian blizzards. Hans had written her of the howling winds and whiteouts of the North Dakota winters of the past, of the cold that cracked trees and killed anyone careless enough to be caught out in it. Her homeland and North Dakota had one thing in common—winter could be deadly.

She shivered at the thought. Was that why Hans had not been back in town? Had there been a terrible blizzard? She shook her head. This new snow was only ankle deep and while snowbanks lined the street, there did not appear to be deep drifts of snow.

Oscar puffed beside her. Nora wished she could repossess her bag but she hated to hurt the man's feelings. He had been so kind to her.

"Here we are," he said. He opened a gate on their left and walked up a path to a porch that spanned the entire front of the house. Oscar stepped forward and, after setting her bag down, thumped on the door.

Nora felt like crawling over the porch railing and hiding down under the straw banking the sides of the house. How terrible to wake people in the middle of the night like this. And bringing a stranger, at that.

"Don't worry, Miss," Oscar turned to her with a smile. It was as if he had read her mind. "The Moens, they'd skin me alive if I didn't bring you here. You needn't worry about your welcome. And they'll probably know about your young man, too." He pounded on the door again.

Nora flinched at each thump of his fist. A light flickered and gleamed beyond the curtain-covered window.

"I'm coming." A deep voice sent shivers up her spine.

Dear Lord, please make this man willing to take me in. I don't know where else I could go this night. She banished thoughts of "no room at the inn" and swallowed hard. This certainly was not going the way Hans's letters had promised, or like her daydreams on the long trip.

The door swung open and a tall man wearing a dark, belted robe shielded the flame of the candle from the wind. "Come in, come in. You must be freezing out there." He stepped back and held the candle high. "Oscar, whom have you brought us this time?"

"Who is it, dear?" A woman's voice floated down from the hall.

"Hello. I'm John Moen, pastor of the Lutheran church here in Soldall." He shut the door behind them and extended a hand to Nora. "That voice you heard, that's my wife, Ingeborge. She'll join us in a minute. And you are . . . ?"

Nora could not decide whether to shake hands with her mittens on or take them off first. She drew off the right one and extended her hand. "I'm Nora Johanson, from Bergen, Norway. I've come—"

"And who is this?" A tiny, rounded woman with her blond hair in a long braid down her back, beamed up at Nora. Her smile removed any doubt of trespassing on their hospitality. "Whom did you bring us, Oscar?"

"I'm sure they'd tell us, if you'd give them a chance." Reverend Moen said, with a twinkle in his eye and love in his voice.

Ingeborge laughed, a merry sound that not only invited smiles from those around but made resistance impossible.

Nora felt a sigh start down in her toes and bubble upward to bring a quiver to her bottom lip. "I . . . I'm Nora Johanson, from Bergen, Norway. My betrothed, Hans Larson was supposed to meet me at the train but I suffered all kinds of delays during my trip here. I wired him a message, but—"

"But he didn't pick it up." Oscar finished for her. "I hoped she could stay here until we notify her young man."

"Yah, sure, you know that she can."

Nora intercepted a look between husband and wife. "Only for tonight," she said, feeling a sharp stab of unease. "I'm sure I can find transportation out to Hans's farm tomorrow. I don't want to cause you any trouble."

"No, it's no trouble." Ingeborge shot another look at her husband and reached up to unwind Nora's long knitted scarf. "You give me your coat and come on over by the fire. Oscar, would you like a cup of coffee before you start home?"

"No, no, that's fine. I need to get along. It's late." He turned to leave and paused. "Is something wrong?"

"I'm afraid so." John studied the floor for a moment, then looked at his wife. At her nod, he continued. "You said you were engaged to Hans Larson?"

Nora nodded. A tiny arrow of fear sneaked between her ribs, stabbing her heart.

Ingeborge reached out to take both of Nora's hands in hers.

"I'm so sorry to be the one to tell you this," John paused again as if fighting to get the words out. "But we buried Hans two days ago. He died of the fever."

two

"It won't be much longer now." Doctor Harmon looked up at Carl Detschman, the pacing father-to-be. "If'n ya can't stand still, get on out to the other room. You men are all alike. You say you want to help and then you make matters worse."

"I'm sorry." The tall man with eyes the faded blue of sun-bleached skies tore his fingers through his thatch of wheaten hair. "I just never—"

"That's the problem, you men never—and I never shoulda asked you to help but Anna here insisted. I shoulda stayed by my rule—no men ever in the birthing room. Go on out and tend your cows or something."

"But this," Carl waved his hand at the woman he loved, the woman who had now been in labor for a day and a night. "How much more can she stand?" Torn between leaving like the doctor said or staying to help if he could, Carl resumed his pacing.

At a groan from his patient, the doctor stopped lecturing the man and turned back to the woman lying limp on the bed, slowly recovering from the small dose of laudanum he had administered to her.

"All right, my dear. You've had a bit of a rest now so let's get this baby born." The doc handed a dry towel to Carl as the younger man dropped back to the bedside to take his wife's hand.

"Anna, my heart, you must be strong," Carl

murmured as he wiped her brow and smoothed back the tousled hair from her white forehead. Fear nearly strangled him at the sight of her slowly opening eyes, now sunken back in her head.

"Carl!" With the attack of another contraction, her hot hands gripped his. Her body arched off the mattress. She bit back the scream that twisted her face in agony. Even in her near-delirium, she kept quiet so she wouldn't waken their three-year-old daughter who slept peacefully in her own room.

"Oh, my God!" Carl said in a prayer. He knew that, in spite of his great physical strength, there was nothing else he could do but pray.

"Push! Push!" The doctor shook his head when he realized his words failed to penetrate the fog she swam in. "Prop her up on the pillows. When the next contraction begins, you yell 'Push' at her and give her every bit of strength you have. I can see the head—if you can just give her the strength to make it through this. You understand?"

Carl nodded and placed his hand on his wife's bulging belly. "Come now, Anna, my love. This is the time." He kept up the soothing murmur even as he felt the contraction begin.

"Now," the doctor ordered when Anna's body tightened again.

"Anna! Push, now! Like you've never done before. Push, Anna!" Carl felt her fingernails dig into the palms of his hands. Her teeth ground into the rag the doctor had placed between her jaws. Sweat poured into her eyes and down to her ears. *God, please! Help us!* He was not sure if he had shouted the plea aloud or screamed it in the hollows of his mind but, at that very second, the doctor grunted his approval.

"You can rest now, my dear." The doctor held the slippery infant in his hands. "You have a son."

Carl leaned his cheek down on Anna's forehead. "You did it, my beautiful love, you did it. You wanted a baby boy and now he is yours." He kissed her forehead, then her cheek.

"Come on, little one, breathe." Doctor Harmon slapped the baby on the buttocks. "Breathe!"

"Wha . . . what's happening?" Anna's voice was so weak, Carl nearly missed it.

"Nothing, everything's fine. You just rest now." Carl murmured reassurances, all the while never taking his eyes from the battle waging at the end of the bed.

The doctor turned the baby over and rubbed its back. Finally, he pinched the minute nose and blew into the baby's mouth.

A cough, faint but gurgling. A moment of silence and then a weak, indignant cry.

"Stubborn, just like his father." Doctor Harmon's shoulders slumped. He placed the infant on Anna's chest and proceeded to cut the umbilical cord, all the while murmuring in a singsong voice.

Carl was not sure if the man was comforting the baby, the mother, or him but he did not care. He finally allowed his shoulders to relax and the tears to flow. They had made it; they had a son. He knelt by the bed and gently touched the baby's head. He wrapped his other arm around Anna's head.

"Is he all right?" Her voice barely stirred the heavy air.

"Yah. He's fine."

Her eyes fluttered open. One hand crept up to lie across the tiny back. "He's so still."

"Resting like you must." Carl stroked her hair back from her forehead.

"Not yet," the doctor said. He picked up the slippery baby and wrapped him in a soft blanket. "Here, Carl. You put him in the cradle by the fire. We, Anna and I, have more work to do here."

Carl pushed himself to his feet and took his tiny son from the doctor's hands. How could anything so small cause such problems for his mother and yet be so perfect?

"All right, now. Let's get this over with." The doctor had no sooner finished saying the words when, along with the afterbirth, came a bright red flood that drenched the sheets.

No matter what he did, the bleeding refused to slow. No matter how desperately Carl pleaded with her to hang on and railed at the doctor to do something, nothing helped. Within a few minutes, Anna Detschman quietly slipped away. She never woke again to cuddle the son she had wanted so much.

Carl sat numbly by as she breathed her last. A pain—the likes of which he had never known before, clogged his throat, his chest, his very life. This could not be happening. Just yesterday, his Anna had been laughing, promising Kaaren a new baby brother. And now. . . .

"I'm so sorry, son." The doctor leaned his head

against the wall. "I don't know what else I could have done." He turned and, bending over, gently pulled the sheet up over Anna's now peaceful face.

Carl folded the sheet back down. "Just leave us alone." His manners caught up with him. "Please."

"Of course." The doctor turned toward the door, then went to the fireplace and picked up the cradle. "I'll wait outside." He left the room, closing the door behind him.

Carl sat on the bed staring at his wife, his love. Only moments ago, she had been there, fighting for the life of their son, and now . . . now she was gone. Anna, the laughing center of his life . . . of their home and family. Gone, leaving him and their children behind. With a gentle finger, he stroked her hand and her pale cheek.

"Oh, Anna. How could you leave me? What kind of a God would let you suffer so and then take you away when we need you so desperately?" He raised his eyes to the ceiling. "Why?" Sobs racked his body as he put his arms around her shoulders and clutched her to his chest. Together they rocked as if he could bring back her life force by sheer willpower.

An hour—an eon later—Carl staggered from the room and collapsed into the rocking chair by the stove. A striped gray cat left the warmth of her box behind the iron stove and rubbed against his leg.

"What will you do?" Doctor Harmon asked from the shadows of the other rocker.

Carl dropped his hand from his eyes and peered into the shadows. "Oh, Doctor Harmon. I . . . I'm sorry. I guess I forgot you were here." His own voice sounded like it came from a far distance.

"I understand." Before he spoke again, the doctor allowed the silence to lengthen. "Oh, Carl, if only I knew of ways to keep tragedies like this from happening. I want you to know how terribly sorry I am."

Carl nodded. "Yah. I know."

"I know you can hardly think now, but that baby there needs some nourishment and soon. Do you know if Anna had some bottles ready. You know, just in case . . . ah . . . of an emergency."

Carl lifted his head. The weight of it took all his strength. "I . . . umm. . . . " His breath sighed out like the bellows of a forge. He waited as if expecting someone else to answer. "I don't know."

Just then, a weak wail grabbed their attention.

"See what I mean?" Doctor Harmon touched the cradle with his foot. "Where would the bottles be?" He spoke slowly and precisely, enunciating each syllable as if Carl were hard of hearing.

"In the pantry, there . . . the door to your left."

"And the milk?"

"Out in the well house." Carl rose from his chair and stumbled to the outside door. He slid his feet into the boots waiting on the rug by the door and lifted his coat from the hook. After pulling a knitted stocking cap over his ears, he turned the knob on the door.

"Don't you need a lantern?" the doctor asked.

"Oh, yes." Carl placed the palm of his hand on the door jamb and leaned his forehead against it. He felt like he was lost in the dark and someone had just blown out the only light.

"Would you like me to get the milk?" Doctor Harmon left his chair and came to stand by the door.

"No. No, I'll be . . . I'll get it."

The baby wailed again, louder this time.

"You see to him, all right?" Carl dug a match out of the box and lit the lantern sitting on the shelf. Without another word, he pulled the door open and staggered out into the dark.

Icy pellets of snow drilled his face and swirled about in the lantern's glow. He kicked the drifted snow away from the well house door and yanked it open. Compared to the freezing wind outside, the cool house felt warm. He pulled a bucket of milk from the nearly frozen water and, after latching the door, headed back to the house.

The doctor, with the swaddled baby in the crook of his arm, had stirred the embers of the fire and added more coal to it. "Water from the reservoir's still warm," he said as he looked up to greet Carl. "I think a cup of coffee would do us both good."

Carl blew out the lantern and hung up his jacket. Bathed in the golden glow from the kerosene lamp on the table, the doctor looked right at home. Carl filled the bottle on the table and set it in the pan of water the doctor had placed off to the side of the range.

When the baby began to fuss, the doctor patted his back and crooned a song in rhythm with the gentle swaying of his own body. "Here," he said, when the bottle seemed warm enough. He handed both baby and bottle to Carl and nodded toward the rocker. "Set yourself down. You both need the rest."

Carl settled down and pushed the nipple into the tiny, rosebud mouth. The baby pushed it out and turned his head, searching for a breast. After several more failed attempts, Carl handed the baby back to the doctor. "You try." He flung himself out of the chair and went to stand at the frosted window.

The baby began to cry, a soft sound that quickly grew into a wail. A voice from the back bedroom joined in the chorus. "Pa-a-a. Ma-a-a."

Carl shrugged his shoulders and dropped his hands in defeat. "Coming Kaaren." He strode down the hall. "It's all right, *liebchen*." He sat on the bed and hugged his three-year-old daughter close. "There's nothing to be afraid of."

"Where's Ma?" the tow-headed child sniffed and rubbed her hand across her eyes. "I want my ma."

Carl hugged her close. "Your ma's busy," he whispered. "You have a new baby brother."

"Ummm." Kaaren nestled into his chest. She popped a thumb into her mouth and, after one pull, relaxed into the sleep of the innocent.

Carl laid her back down. He could still hear the baby crying.

"He refuses to suck on this thing." The doctor waved the bottle in the lamplight. "He won't last long if he doesn't eat."

"Do you know anyone who could wet-nurse him?" asked Carl.

The doctor shook his head and tried again to get the infant to take the bottle.

Carl raked his fingers through his hair until the white blond strands stood straight up. "What am I going to do?"

The doctor pushed himself to his feet. "How about harnessing up my horse while I rewarm this and try again. I'll get to town right about sunrise and I'll see if I can find one of the women to come out and help you. They're always better at this than I am. Maybe widow Nelson can help. Naah. She's gone to Fargo to take care of her sister."

Carl ignored the doctor's mutterings and dressed again for the cold outside. Lantern in hand, he opened the door and left, shutting it quickly to keep out the cold.

The barn warmth welcomed him as he slipped in through the small door. The doctor's old bay horse nickered a greeting. Even that simple touch brought the tears to Carl's eyes. To keep from throwing himself down on the mound of hay and letting the tears ravage him, he concentrated on each step of the job at hand.

Pick up the harness, settle the leathers in place, buckle the straps, and lead the animal out of the stall. Back the gelding between the shafts, "Sooo now, easy, boy." *Don't think. Don't feel.*

Why was he so clumsy? Because of his gloves? He dashed the back of the knitted fabric across his eyes.

Secure the shafts to the breast piece. Open the main double doors. He continued giving himself orders, as if all this was new to him. Then, he backed the horse and buggy out into the freezing wind. After retrieving his lantern and closing the door, he led the horse up to the house.

He trudged along, knowing he would rather have stayed in the barn. In there, life was as it should be. Life, not death. But duty called him back to the house.

Carl blocked the thought of his wife lying in their bed.

Think of something else. Think of nothing.

The house was silent.

"Shhh." The doctor laid a finger across his lips. He was dressed for the outdoors, his hat pulled down, over his ears. "He's asleep." He pointed to a cradle by the stove. "I got him to take a bit. I'll try to find someone for you. In the meantime, try giving him some each time he wakes up. If he gets hungry enough, maybe he'll eat."

"Thank you, Doctor." Carl extended his hand. The older man clasped it and covered their joined hands with his other.

"You're welcome, son. I just wish I coulda done more." The man hefted his worn black bag and slipped out the door.

Carl listened to the jingle of the harness as the horse trotted down the lane. Only the whistle of the wind, seeking entrance through tiny cracks, disturbed the silence of the house. The awful silence.

three

Nora felt like a glacier pressed upon her shoulders.

"Oh, my dear, I am so sorry." Ingeborge guided the younger woman into a chair. "Such terrible news and right off when you first arrive like this." She pulled up a stool and perched immediately in front of her guest so as to hold Nora's shaking hands.

Nora heard the men talking by the door as from a great distance. She forced herself to concentrate on the caring woman before her. What had she said? Anything that needed an answer? Hans had died. He was dead. Shouldn't she be weeping? But the sorrow was more like that of losing a dear friend, not the love of one's life. She was sad. Of course. But it did not seem to touch her—not inside where heart and love dwelled.

Instead, the thoughts that set her body shaking raced one on top of the other. *What ever would she do now? Wherever would she go? Who would take care of Hans's farm? Could she live there?* She pulled herself back from looking over the precipice of her future and focused on the tender smile of the woman in front of her.

"I . . . I'm sorry, I seemed to have wandered off somewhere." Nora leaned back in the chair and drew in a deep breath. She felt the shudder start at her toes and work its way up until even her teeth rattled.

31

"Are you cold? Can I get you a blanket? The coffee will be ready shortly." Ingeborge rubbed Nora's icy hands.

Nora heard the door close and Reverend Moen approach. She studied her hands, warmly clasped in Ingeborge's, as if to keep the outer world at bay. Her own hands, so large with long fingers and so smooth due to the long weeks of idleness. Ingeborge's hands, small and reddened from the work of her house. Maybe she could help the Moens for a time.

But Hans's cows and the horses. Who was taking care of them since he had passed away? He had said he had no near neighbors.

She reached to unbutton her coat. Here she was, dripping all over the spotless kitchen. What kind of visitor did things like that?

"I'm sorry for dripping snow on your floor. What you must think of me."

"No, no. You mustn't worry. You've had a great shock. Here, let me take that." Ingeborge pulled herself to her feet and reached for Nora's dark, wool coat. "Let me hang this over a chair by the stove so it can dry. Your scarf and mittens, too."

Nora felt like a small child obeying her mother. How comforting. She went through the motions but her mind insisted on darting around like a cornered animal. Hans—her friend of so many years—was gone. When she thought of their growing up together, she felt the tears beginning in the back of her throat. What about his parents? At the thought of their dear faces, the tears overflowed.

She covered her face with her hands, trying to

stifle the sobs that shook her shoulders. Oh, the dreams that died along with a loved one. The happinesses that now would never be.

She felt a hand smoothing her hair, heard a gentle voice murmuring condolences. Words that ran together with no meaning, save that of love. She rested in their comfort.

When Nora leaned her weary head against the back of the chair, Ingeborge took a steaming cup of coffee from her husband and handed it to the young woman. "Drink this, it will help. I don't know if you use sugar but I sweetened it to lick the shock."

Nora nodded her thanks and wrapped her hands around the mug. She sipped carefully. The aroma seeped into her pores, as the warmth cupped between both her hands and now sliding down her throat overcame the shivers.

"Did you know Hans well?" She looked from one Moen to the other.

Reverend Moen nodded. "We knew him, but we were not what you might call friends. He attended our church a few times when he had first arrived. This is a small community so everyone knows everyone else."

"Did he talk much about his farm . . . our farm? You see, I'm concerned about the cows and horses, that someone is caring for them." Nora caught one of those looks pass from husband to wife again. An uncomfortable silence thrummed between the three of them. Nora took her courage in hand. "Is something else wrong?"

Reverend Moen inhaled deeply. "You asked about

his farm?"

Nora nodded. "Hans wrote in his letters, about the two-storied house and big barn, three milk cows, and a team of gray horses he'd already purchased. He said that last year he built a windmill so I wouldn't even have to pump water. He said. . . ." Her voice trailed off. She had been babbling like a brook in the spring. She rubbed the smooth edge of the cup in her hand.

"Ach, you poor child." Ingeborge patted Nora's knee.

"Please, tell me." Nora whispered her plea.

Reverend Moen drew up a straight-backed kitchen chair and folded his lean frame down onto it. He shook his head. "I am so sorry to be the bearer of bad news tonight but . . . well. . . ." He drew in another deep breath. "Hans Larson worked as a farmhand for the Elmer Peterson family, south of town. He lived in their bunkhouse with the other hired hands." He shook his head. "Hans didn't even own the horse he rode."

This is too much. I cannot bear all this. Nora's thoughts weighed her down. She wished she could sink through the leather seat of the rocker and down into the floor. "Are you . . . you sure? My Hans Larson was tall, yellow hair, and a smile that broke your heart. He. . . ." She forced her mind to think of something different about him. "He had a scar from a burn on the back of his right hand, from when we were children."

Reverend Moen nodded. "Yes, that's whom I am talking about. The same Hans Larson, from Bergen,

Norway. He arrived about three years ago."

The crushing iceberg settled on her again. Nora bit the inside of her lip to keep it from quivering. No Hans. No farm. "Well, then, at least there are no animals suffering from neglect." She attempted a smile in the minister's direction but failed miserably.

Instead, she studied the muted colors in the braided rug at her feet. Anything was better than looking at the faces of the two sympathetic Moens. How could she have been such a fool?

"You mustn't blame yourself . . . I mean . . . how could you have known anything else clear back in Norway? You trusted his letters, like you should have." Ingeborge leaned forward from her perch on the stool. "Besides, he was such a charming young man."

That he was, thought Nora. His charm was one reason she had fallen in love with him. Or had she fallen in love with love, with the adventure of coming to the New World? She drank some more of the sweet coffee; its warmth seemed to melt that glacier she felt resting on her. After draining the coffee mug, she glanced around for a place to set it down.

Ingeborge took the empty cup. "Would you like some more?"

Nora shook her head.

"Then, if you'd like, I will show you to your bed. I'm afraid you must share it with our seven-year-old Mary. She'll be surprised when she wakes up in the morning, but Mary loves company."

Nora felt the words flowing over her like a healing draft. She did not have to make any decisions tonight. Maybe tomorrow she would be able to think better. Maybe tomorrow God would work a miracle and take this all away. Maybe tomorrow she would awaken from this terrible dream and be back with her beloved family.

"Good night, then," she nodded to the man adjusting the damper in the great black iron stove. "And, thank you."

"I've already taken your bag upstairs." He clattered the round lid of the stove back into place. "Sleep well. Things always have a way of looking brighter in the morning, even when times seem the darkest."

"*Mange takk.*" Nora followed Ingeborge up the steep stairs. Halfway up she paused to rest. She had not realized how exhausted she was. Each step seemed like a mountain, with her feet so weighted she could barely lift them. She stepped with her right foot, then her left, each dragging the other until she reached the upper hall. Soft light, from Ingeborge's candle, beckoned from the room on the left.

"If you sit in that rocking chair, I can help you with your boots." Ingeborge turned from arranging the sleeping child in the bed. "Have you a nightgown in your bag?"

Nora nodded as she sank down into the chair. Waves of weary sadness washed over her. She felt like she had been pounded by waves down in the fjord on a stormy day and was being pulled out to sea. Ingeborge's voice came from far away. She felt herself sinking.

"Now, let's just get you in bed before you fall asleep in the chair." A gentle hand tugged her upright. Nora did as the voice commanded. She stood, stepped, turned, and sank into the featherbed that rose up to greet her. She heard her mother's voice, *"Now mind your manners,"* but Nora could not force the required *"Mange takk"* past the sleep that clogged her throat and eyes.

"God bless you, my dear. I'll leave the candle here in case you need it." Ingeborge smoothed the hair back from Nora's forehead just like she had done to her daughter. The feather-light touch was the last sensation Nora felt; she was at home, in her mother's care.

Light, bright as though from a thousand flashing diamonds, filled her eyes. She blinked against the brightness, then slowly opened her eyelids. To the left, sun streaming through the frosted window pane made her blink again. She turned her head to the right.

A solemn stare from bright blue eyes met her own. In a blur of spinning braids and a voice to wake the deaf, the child fled out the door.

"Ma, she's awake!" echoed in the hall.

Nora stretched her hands over her head and pointed her toes to the end of the mattress. Oh, how good it felt as she rotated her shoulders.

The night before came crashing back. Hans was dead. Hans had lied. What was she to do now? She felt like pulling the covers over her head to blot out the sun and the new day. Instead, she lifted her head and looked around the room. Covered by colorful patchwork quilts, she had not noticed the cold through the night. A small rocker held a rag doll, that kept company with the grownup one. By the bed, a pitcher and matching bowl painted with pink roses sat on top of a dark oak commode. More pink roses climbed trellises up the wallpapered walls . . . the same pink roses she had dreamed of for her new home.

"Enough of that," she ordered herself when she could feel a lump beginning in her throat. "As Ma always says, 'The good Lord has His eye on the sparrow and us as well.' " She threw back the covers and planted her feet firmly on the braided rug of many colors. "This is the day that the Lord hath made. I will rejoice and be glad in it."

She bit back the quiver in her chin. She had said that verse every morning since her confirmation, but today it was difficult to say. So she said it again—more firmly. "This is the day that the Lord hath made." She heard footsteps coming up the stairs. "I will rejoice and be glad in it."

Ingeborge tapped on the door before entering. "What a marvelous way to start the day." Cheeks red from the heat of the cooking stove made her blue eyes sparkle even more. "You must have been sleeping hard since Mary came down without waking you."

"Oh, I did . . . sleep well, that is."

Ingeborge poured hot water into the pitcher on the stand. "Now you can wash and, when you're ready, there's breakfast waiting."

"Ma. . . ." A young voice floated up the stairwell.

"That's Knute. He's five. You've met Mary. . . . "

Nora nodded.

"Ma-a-a."

"Goodness. With these four of mine there's always something." She turned in a swirl of skirts but paused at the door. "You come down when you're ready now."

Nora pressed a hand to her chest and shook her head. She felt like a whirlwind had just blown through the room. She crossed the room and closed the door. Now, she would finally have a real washing.

In spite of the heating grate in the floor, she shivered in the cold room as she hurried through her bathing. Wishing for clean clothes, she thought of her trunk still at the station. But that would come later. She pulled on her clothes and the long black wool stockings. While warmer, she no longer felt so clean. She shook out her shirtwaist and black wool skirt before buttoning them in place.

With her hair brushed and rebraided she felt more like a young woman who had boarded the train for a new country. Actually, she was feeling better than she had felt for days. In spite of her difficulties, she hummed under her breath while she made the bed and wiped the water from the oak stand.

As she made her way down the stairs, she could hear young voices. Her stomach rumbled, reminding her of how long it had been since her last meal.

She turned to the right and stopped at the entry to

the kitchen. Two children sat at the oval oak table in front of the window, reading their lessons. They looked up when they heard her tread. Nora smiled at them both and then at the picture Ingeborge made. The baby nestled in her arms while a chubby little girl played with the cat at her mother's feet.

An ache began somewhere in the middle of Nora's heart. This was what she had dreamed of . . . and now that dream was shattered. She resecured the smile on her face and buried the ache under the ashes of her yesterday. As Ma and the Good Book said, "Sorrow reigns at night, but joy cometh in the morning."

And this was definitely morning—she glanced at the grandfather clock by the door—but not morning for much longer.

"I'm sorry to be such a lazybones, I. . . ."

"Not at all." Ingeborge shook her head. "You needed the rest. Now, I know you must be starved." When she started to get up, Nora laid a hand on the woman's shoulder.

"No, you stay there with the baby. Just tell me where things are and I will fix my own. The coffee smells wonderful." She reached into the glass-faced cupboard for a cup. A loaf of bread sat on the counter, next to a crock of jam.

"Thank you, my dear. Everything is right in front of you. We'll be having soup for dinner in about an hour or when Reverend Moen returns. He had some calls to make."

While Nora sliced the homemade bread, Ingeborge introduced her children. "Mary is the oldest at seven, Knute is five, Grace is three, and James here is five months." She dropped a kiss on the rosy cheek of the baby asleep in her arms. The gentle rocking of the chair creaked its own song, in counterpoint with the kettle singing on the stove.

Nora sighed blissfully as she took her first sip of coffee and bite of the jellied bread. She placed two thick slices on a plate and carried her breakfast over to the table. "Do you mind if I join you?" she asked the children.

The two with hair so blond as to be white, hers in braids and his bowl-cut, stared at her solemnly. Mary broke the ice with a grin. "I didn't think you were ever going to wake up."

Not to be outdone, Knute piped up. "Did you like the train ride?"

"He always wants to go on the train." Mary closed her book. "But we never have." She leaned her chin on her stacked fists. "Ma said you went on a ship, too."

Nora set her plate and cup on the table, then pulled out a high-backed oak chair. "Yes, I did. Both a ship and a train." She sat down. "Now, why do you like the train so?" She leaned forward to look Knute right in the eyes.

"It is so big and goes so fast."

"Big and fast. Big and fast." Mary shook her head like big sisters everywhere.

Nora smothered a grin behind her coffee cup. "Someday, I'm sure you'll have a train ride."

"Now, you children go play in the other room," their mother ordered. She rose to her feet and laid the baby in his cradle. "Miss Johanson and I would like to visit."

"Yes, Ma." The two obediently slid to the floor and, gathering their books, ran laughing down the hall.

"No running in the house."

"Yes, Ma." A giggle floated back to the peaceful room.

Ingeborg poured herself a cup of coffee and brought it over to the table. The orange striped cat followed her and wound herself around Nora's ankles. The toddler followed the cat and tugged at her mother's skirt to be picked up.

Nora felt a tug at her heart. "What beautiful children you have." She leaned over and scratched along the cat's arched back. "It is so wonderful here."

"Thank you." Ingeborge settled little Grace on her lap and leaned back in her chair. "Mary and Knute should be at school but there have been so many children sick that they closed the school for a time. I thank the Lord each day for keeping us safe and healthy. The fever seems to come like a fiend from the north and before you realize it, people are coughing to death. That's where John is now. Someone else died during the night. And the doctor was at a difficult birthing. But there seems to be nothing he can do for these poor ones. Some get well but many don't."

"We've had those in Norway, too. But not so much this last year." Nora got up and refilled her coffee cup.

"Ach, what a terrible hostess I am," Ingeborge moved as if to get up.

"No, you stay there. This is the least I can do when you take in a stranger like this." Nora sat back down. The cat leaped up into her lap and settled itself for a nap.

"The cat likes you; the children like you; I like you. That means we all agree. You are welcome to stay as long as you need to." Ingeborge stroked little Grace's silky white hair; the little one's eyes drooped closed and a thumb found it's way into her mouth.

"You have no idea how much your offer means to me but I must earn my own way. With all the illness, isn't there someone who needs a strong back and willing hands?"

"I don't know." The older woman wrinkled her brow in thought. "Can you teach school? There is a town not far from here that is looking for a school-teacher.

Nora shook her head. "I think not. I have no certificate and besides, I don't speak English. Does everyone around here speak Norwegian?"

"No, there are Germans and Swedes and several Norse dialects. You would have to learn English." She thought a while. "You're not thinking of return-ing to Norway then?"

"I have no money."

"None at all?"

"Four pennies. That is why Oscar brought me here last night. I couldn't afford the hotel." Nora sipped her coffee. "Do you suppose they need anyone at the hotel? I can cook and clean."

Ingeborge shuddered. "I know the Lord says not to speak ill of anyone but we can't let you work there. We'll ask John when he comes home. Surely he'll have an idea of what to do."

Nora stroked the soft fur of the cat purring in her lap. It was true, animals and children always took to her, especially the wounded. Back home she loved teaching Sunday School for the little ones. If only she did not need English to teach school in North Dakota.

The clock bonged the first notes of twelve.

"Oh, my land. John may be home any minute." Ingeborge roused the sleepy Grace and, after a quick kiss, set the child on the floor. "Mary, time to set the table. Knute, the coal bin is nearly empty."

"Let me help." Nora set the cat down in Grace's arms and patted the little girl on the head. She glanced out the window. "Here comes Reverend Moen. He's just opening the gate."

Nora helped Mary set the table and, with everyone flying to do their jobs, the dinner was on the table by the time the father had hung his coat on the coat rack by the door and had washed his hands. The children scrambled into their places, Grace into her highchair and, when the adults sat down, everyone joined hands for grace.

The familiar words of the table prayer transported Nora back to the warm kitchen of her family's farm. She swallowed a tear and sneaked a peak at the child in the highchair beside her.

Grace murmured her own unintelligible words

along with them all. But her "Ah-men" rang loud
and clear and her proud grin prompted giggles from
the others.

Their father eyed them sternly but they caught the
twitch in his cheek.

Nora tried to suffocate her chortle but a glance at
Ingeborge struggling the same way, did her in.

When they all laughed, Grace announced "Ahh-
men" again and banged her spoon on the table.

Reverend Moen reached over and removed the
spoon from the child's hand. "Yah, that was good."
He smoothed her hair back with the back of his
knuckles. "Now you must eat your dinner like
Mama's good little girl." He looked around the
table. "As you all must."

Conversation lagged while everyone devoured the
soup, both first and second helpings. When they
finished, Ingeborge brought cookies and coffee to
the table.

"Now. Did Mary and Knute do all their lessons?"
Reverend Moen gazed at each child, then his wife.

"Mostly." Mary answered.

"That's not enough. You go get your books and
bring them to the table while we talk. Knute's, too."
When the children were settled and the coffee
poured, he turned to Nora. "And now, how are
you?"

"I'll be all right. This all takes some getting used
to."

"Yes, it does. I want you to know you can remain
with us as long as you want."

"*Mange takk.* But we, Ingeborge and I, were

talking about—do you know anyone who needs a . . . someone like me to help them? Ingeborge said you might have heard of someone who is sick or a family that needs . . . well, I can cook and clean, manage a house, a barn." Her voice began to fade away. She took a breath. "I'm not afraid of work."

Reverend Moen leaned back against the chair. He looked up at the ceiling, his brow creased in thought. The clock ticked loudly in the silence. "There are so many that need help but they can't afford to pay anyone. Times are harsh here on the prairie." He rubbed the bridge of his nose with a long finger. "I'll ask Doctor Harmon if I see him this afternoon. We'll be having another funeral in the morning. Old Peder Stroenven died during the night."

"Ach, this is so hard." Ingeborge shook her head. "The young and the old are always hit the hardest."

Nora glanced out the window in time to see a horse and sleigh stop in front of the gate. "You have company."

Reverend Moen pushed back his chair and rose to his feet. "You'd best make some more coffee. Whoever it is will be cold clear through if he's driven far. The cold is fierce even with the sun shining."

He strode to the door and pulled it open before the knock sounded. "Why, Carl Detschman. How good to see you. Come right in."

Nora felt lost immediately. The greeting was in English. She looked up to find frozen blue eyes staring at her. Then the man's gaze flickered back to the pastor. Their conversation continued.

The man handed a well-wrapped bundle to Ingeborge and pushed a very young girl forward also. Then he touched his hand to his forehead and left. The door closed behind him.

"Oh, the poor man." Ingeborge sank down in a chair and began to unwrap the bundle. A tiny red-faced infant emitted a wavering cry. Tears formed in the little girl's blue eyes and ran down her cheeks.

"Pa!" she cried and ran to the door. "Pa!"

"What is it? Can I help?" Nora sprang to her feet.

Ingeborge settled herself in the rocker. "Carl's wife died last night in childbirth and he can't get this mite to take a bottle. John said we'd help. Why don't you bring the little girl here. Her name is Kaaren."

"Now, we'll have two funerals tomorrow." Reverend Moen stood in front of the window. "Dear Lord, when will this cease?"

I wonder if this is the family I am to help, Nora thought as she went to the stove for the coffeepot. *Mr. Detschman is certainly a man with more than his share of troubles.*

four

"Oh, that poor man." Nora felt her heart break for him.

"Pa-a-a." Kaaren tried turning the doorknob to follow her father. Tears streamed down her face as she twisted on the slippery knob.

Nora rose and knelt by the child. "Your pa will come back. Come here and let me dry your tears."

Kaaren pulled away and wailed more loudly.

Nora sat back on her heels. If only she could speak the language.

Reverend Moen stooped beside her. "Come, Kaaren, you must give this up now. You'll make yourself sick with such tears." He lifted the little girl in his arms and patted her back.

"Pa, I . . . I want my . . . my pa."

Nora rose to her feet, thankful that the Moens spoke both Norwegian and English. However would she be able to work for a family that did not speak Norwegian?

"Mary, you take Kaaren and show her your dolls," John said. He set the crying child down again and linked the two girls hands. "Kaaren, you go with Mary. Knute, why don't you help entertain our visitor, also?" When the children wandered off to the other room chattering, he turned to Nora.

"Carl said he needed to get back to take care of his livestock. That's why he left so hastily. He also said he'd bring Anna, that's his wife, in for the funeral tomorrow."

"Oh, that poor, poor man." Nora shook her head. Visions of stern, blue eyes in a strongly handsome face returned to her. So young for such a tragedy. She totally forgot her own situation while praying for his.

"God be thanked that Carl didn't lose his son, too," Ingeborge added.

"That is true. But for right now. . . . " Reverend Moen studied the toe of his boot. He inhaled deeply and sighed in weariness. "I need to go over to the blacksmith and ask him to prepare another box. Then locate someone to ride out and help Carl. He looked about at the end of his tether." Reverend Moen reached for his coat and hat. He paused. "You know anyone besides yourself who could wet-nurse this baby, Inge?"

Ingeborge looked up. "What? Oh dear, I don't know, not right now."

After the man left the house, Nora began clearing the table. Had the good Lord answered her prayer already? Here was someone, literally on their doorstep, who needed help. And he needed help now! Granted, she could not nurse the baby but maybe she could persuade him to take a bottle. Maybe after Ingeborge nursed him a few times to get his strength up—the thoughts leaped and tumbled over one another.

"There, now," Ingeborge said with a sigh of relief. "The mite finally found out what he's supposed to do." She pushed her rocker into its creaking song.

"Who else might still be nursing a baby? We've had no newborns around here for a time."

Nora reached under the sink for a metal pan. After slicing several curls off the hard lye soap bar and into the pan, she poured in steaming water from the teakettle. Then, she added the dishes. All the while her thoughts tumbled on. She could work for Carl Detschman, of course she could. That way she would earn money for her passage back to Norway. She could go home. What kind of wages would he pay? Maybe he was unable to pay like the others that Ingeborge mentioned. What then?

Memory of her mother's voice blew cool reason through the confusion in her mind. *"If you are doing God's will, He will make your path straight."* I don't only need it straight, Nora thought, I need the bumps taken out and a good road map. *What am I supposed to do?*

"There." Ingeborge nestled the infant up on her shoulder and rubbed his back for a burp. "He should feel much better now."

"What did they name the baby?" Nora finished drying the dishes and putting them away.

"Peder. Peder Detschman. Such a strong name. He will have much to live up to." The baby burped in her ear. "There now, little one." She cuddled him in the crook of her arm; the rocking chair continued its song.

Nora heard the beginning stirrings of Ingeborge's baby waking in the cradle by the rocker. She hung the dish towel over the bar behind the stove and, picking up the iron handle, lifted the round stove lid and set it to the side. Red coals glowed in the firebox. She picked up the small, metal scoop on top of the coal bucket and dug out several dusty, brown pieces of lignite, the soft coal of North Dakota, and scattered them over the red embers. After replacing the lid, she dropped the scoop back into place.

The baby in the cradle announced that he was ready to be picked up now—and eat.

"Will you have enough for him?" Nora nodded toward the cradle.

"We'll make do." Ingeborge put both arms around the baby in her arms and made as if to stand. She looked from the bundle in her arms to Nora and then back down. "Here, you take little Peder and lay him in the cradle after I take James in for dry diapers.

Nora leaned over to take the infant from the older woman's arms. As she straightened, she studied the baby wrapped so tightly in his blankets. When his eyelids fluttered and the rosebud mouth yawned, she felt her heart fly right out of her chest and open wide to the tiny baby.

"Oh, you are a darling, baby mine," she crooned to him as she rocked him carefully in her arms. Without a thought, she hummed him a lullabye, learned at her mother's knee. She hesitated to put him down, this mite who was starting life with no mother. He needed her.

If only she had milk for him. But she did not. Her practical side won out and she laid him on his stomach in the cradle.

Peder squirmed and mewed like a newborn kitten. When Nora gently rocked the cradle and resumed her sweet song, his body relaxed and he drifted back to sleep. Nora knelt by the cradle, reluctant to take leave of her charge.

She smiled as Ingeborge returned with her contented baby perched in her arms. James waved an arm and, turning his face, began rooting at his mother's breast.

"Yah, you are hungry again." Ingeborge settled herself back in the rocker. "With the two of these young men, I know what a ewe with twins feels like." His sucks and gurgles proclaimed his relief that he was finally being fed.

Ingeborge chuckled as she stroked the baby's round, still-bald head. "This one, he's not shy about letting his mama know when she is neglecting her duty. He seems so big, especially when I hold him right after little Peder." She trailed a finger down the baby's rosy cheek.

His blue eyes concentrating on his mother's face, James waved a chubby fist and reached for his mother's mouth. She nibbled on his fingers and then kissed them.

Nora felt an ache in her heart. If only she and Hans. . . . She rose to her knees and then to her feet. As she dusted off the back of her skirt, she dusted away the regrets. Hans was now a memory and any dreams of him and their life together should be put to rest in the cold ground, like he had been. That sounded so easy.

"Ingeborge, would you like a cup of coffee?" She swept away the thoughts, firmly planting a smile on her mouth, a mouth that would rather quiver.

"Yes, please. Here I am so remiss. What kind of a hostess do you think I am?"

"A very busy one," Nora replied with a smile. "Since I'm not able to perform your special task, let me take over some of your other ones."

"There are cookies in the round blue tin on the second shelf," Ingeborge motioned to the cupboards with her chin. "Why don't you set out enough for everyone and call the children. They have been playing so good. There's milk for them in the pantry."

Nora did as asked, taking a peek at the sleeping infant every time she passed the cradle. He was so tiny. As soon as the table was set, she walked through the sitting room, scarcely taking time to admire the stiff, horsehair sofa and matching chairs. She could hear the children laughing through a door at the opposite end of the room.

"There are cookies and milk on the table," she said, pausing in the doorway.

Smiles greeted her from the two girls sitting cross-legged on a counterpane, surrounded by dolls. Mary cuddled a porcelain-faced doll with curly, blond hair and dressed in blue dimity. Kaaren clutched a rag doll as if it would be taken from her; she turned to look up at Nora.

On the floor, Knute stopped his train rumblings and screechy noises and sprung to his feet. "Cookies, yumm." He brushed past Nora in the doorway.

"Knute, put your train away," Mary called after him.

As he trudged back into the room muttering under

his breath, Mary took Kaaren's hand. "Come on. There are cookies and milk." When spoken in English so she could understand, Kaaren smiled and, still hugging the doll to her chest, slipped by Nora in the doorway, careful not to touch her—or look at her.

What does she think I am, the big bad troll? Nora thought while waiting for the hurrying boy to put his toys away. Just because I talk Norwegian instead of English. Poor little mite, how will she bear it with no mother? I wonder if they've told her yet. How do you tell a little one like her that her ma won't be coming back anymore? How can she ever understand . . . when I don't?

Nora followed after the children, wishing she could gather little Kaaren close and take away the tears that would be coming.

And come they did, as soon as Kaaren saw Ingeborge nursing her baby, James, in the rocking chair. "I want my ma-a-a." Huge tears spilled from her eyes and rolled down her cheeks. When Mary offered her a cookie, Kaaren pushed it away and continued to cry. She scrubbed her fists into her eyes and leaned her forehead onto the edge of the table.

Nora scooped the little girl up in her arms and sat back down on the vacated chair. She rocked back and forth, cuddling Kaaren against her chest and murmuring words of comfort. She stroked the fine, blond hair and wiped away the tears as they continued to course down the pale cheeks.

"Hush, now," she crooned. "You'll make yourself

sick with all these tears. You've cried so many we'll all float away on a puddle."

Mary left her chair and brought one of the crisp sugar cookies to Kaaren. She took the younger girl's hand and placed the cookie in it. "My ma makes the best cookies anywhere. You'll like this." Mary took a big bite of the cookie in her other hand and grinned between chews. "See?"

Kaaren sniffed back her tears and took a bite. As she solemnly nibbled at the rich cookie, she kept her gaze on Mary. Sniffs punctuated the bites.

Nora looked over the little girl's head to see Ingeborge smiling and nodding. The baby had finished eating and was now playing poke-a-finger-in-my-mother's-mouth, a favorite mother-baby game since time began. She could hear him cooing, imitating his mother's sounds and, once in a while, adding a contagious belly laugh.

She continued the soothing rocking motion and laid her cheek against the child's head leaning on her chest. Who would care for this dear little one? Could it be herself? How would she propose this idea of hers? Just step forward and say "I know you need help with your children and I need work?" She mentally shook her head. Should she talk this over with Ingeborge? But what if she disapproved? Why would she do that? Nora felt like she had two people arguing in her head.

"Mary, why don't you and Kaaren play with James while I start fixing supper? Bring the quilt in from the foot of the bed and all of you can play on the floor." Ingeborge held her baby under his arms and bounced him on her knee. "I could sit and play with you all afternoon and then what would your pa say? He'd like to have supper ready when he comes home." The baby gurgled in agreement.

While the children played on the floor, the women shared the cooking chores. Nora peeled carrots and potatoes to add to the already cooked pot of chicken that Ingeborge had brought in from the pie safe on the screened-in back porch.

"Then, we'll make some dumplings and supper'll be all ready." The older woman glanced at the clock bonging by the door. "We have time to make applesauce cookies. Would you like to help me?"

"Of course." Nora rinsed off her hands and bent over to check the cradle where Peder was making the squeaking noises of a baby awakening. She set the cradle rocking gently with the toe of her shoe. "Hush now, little one. You must sleep longer."

"Yah, so I have more milk for him." Ingeborge set a tan earthenware bowl on the table and began adding ingredients. As she measured and stirred, she kept up a running introduction of the residents of Soldall for Nora's delight and amusement.

Nora felt like she would be able to recognize her prospective neighbors just from Ingeborge's mimicry. "What can you tell me about Carl Detschman?" Nora asked after giggling at another of Ingeborge's tales of life in Soldall.

After sliding a sheet of cookies into the blackened oven, Ingeborge paused. The creak and slam of the oven door snapped her back in motion. "Yah, that poor man. He has his hands full now. And it is so

hard for him to ask for help." She shook her head,
like so many other women who wish they could do
something but did not know what.

Nora waited, continuing to drop the cookie dough
onto another flat baking pan.

"We've known Carl since he arrived in Soldall six
years ago. He was just starting out after buying old
Mr. Einer Peterson's farm. Einer had died that summer, from the consumption. He'd been sick a very
long time."

Nora had a hard time to keep from interrupting.
She did not want to hear about Einer Peterson.

"Carl came from Minnesota, somewhere down by
St. Paul, so he has no family around here. He was
already betrothed; that was such a disappointment
to the young ladies in our church. You could just see
their eyes light up the day he walked into services.
Such a handsome young man."

Nora could agree with that even though she had
seen him when he seemed frozen in the middle of an
ice chunk.

"And the voice of an angel. When he sings those
hymns—why he just lifts the rest of the congregation and leads us into heaven." Ingeborge winked at
Nora then picked up the full sheet of cookies and
slid it onto the bottom rack in the oven. With one
finger, she touched one of the cookies on the top
rack to see if it was done. When the cookie indented
rather than springing back, she turned the cookie
sheet around 180 degrees and closed the oven.
"Now, where was I?"

"About what a voice Carl has." Nora reminded

her.

"Oh yes, and such nice manners. You know his ma taught him well. He brought Anna to meet us when they returned after the wedding. They were married at the end of harvest. It was a very good year, I remember. He'd ordered a new wagon to drive her home in, painted all red and green with shiny yellow wheels. That wagon was really a sight."

Nora did not want to hear about the wagon, either.

"He's a hard worker, that Carl. Einer, because he was so sick, had let the farm run down. But by the next year, Carl had painted the barns and even the house. I said Carl is a hard worker. Well, his Anna was, too. It was a shame they didn't get more acquainted with the community. But, they worked from dawn to dark.

Ingeborge opened the creaky, oven door and removed the top sheet, placing it off to the cool side of the range while she moved the bottom sheet to the upper rack.

"Oh, Ma, those look so good." Mary and her three shadows lined up by the table, ogling the cookies as her mother lifted the fragrant goodies from the pan to the table.

"Wait until they cool a bit." Ingeborge pushed away an inquisitive finger. "My, they do smell good, don't they?" She sniffed appreciatively.

Nora agreed. The apple-cinnamon aroma filled the room. She dug a finger into the dough and, after putting the dab in her mouth, sucked her finger clean. She looked up, guilt evidenced in the heat coating her cheeks when she saw Ingeborge watching her. "I know, I'm setting a bad example for the children as my ma always said, but. . . ."

"No buts, child. I usually can't resist myself. But here, why don't you try this instead?" She picked up a hot cookie and brought it over, along with the empty pan. "You eat this and I'll finish." She turned back to the table. "Go ahead, children. Just be careful you don't burn yourselves." The three did not need a second invitation.

"Thank you," they chorused and joined James back on the quilt.

"No! No! He's too little." Nora flew across the room to scoop the baby up, safe from the cookie Kaaren was going to shove into his mouth.

The little girl burst into tears that turned into wails. "Ma-a-a-a. I want my ma."

Realizing he did not know who the strange person was who had snatched him up, little James joined Kaaren, puckering up and letting loose with a wall-shaking howl.

Mary and Knute stared from one to the other, forgotten cookies clutched in their hands.

Ingeborge dropped the spoon of cookie dough and, in the process of spinning around to help Nora, bumped the cradle with her toe.

With both the noise and motion, Peder yowled almost before he awakened.

"There, there," Nora tried to quiet the screaming baby in her arms with one hand and comfort the little girl with the other.

"Whatever is going on in here?" Reverend Moen stepped through the door. "I could hear the noise clear out to the street."

Ingeborge gathered James from Nora and hid her laughing face in the baby's chubby neck. James quieted immediately.

Mary patted Kaaren on the back, trying to comfort her but to no avail.

Nora looked from the little girl to the baby yelling in the cradle. Whom should she go to first? When Reverend Moen squatted down in front of the two little girls, Nora picked up the screaming infant. She put him up to her shoulder, joggling him and crooning comfort at the same time.

"What's for supper?" John asked after calming Kaaren and picking her up. Together, they leaned over the fresh cookies on the table.

Nora and Ingeborge stared at each other—supper was not ready.

Ingeborge threw her hands into the air and laughed. "Chicken and dumplings but, even with two cooks, it'll be a while."

"I can fix the dumplings since I can't take care of this one's needs." Nora continued swaying with the still-snuffling baby.

"Good." Ingeborge turned to her husband. "And, if you'll take care of your young son here, we can proceed. Mary, why don't you and Kaaren set the table?"

"Oh, the cookies." Nora reached for a pot holder as she handed Ingeborge the baby. The smell of burning chased the cookie fragrance from the room. All the cookies on the back corner of the pan had changed from light brown to smokey black.

"I'm so sorry to burn. . . ." Nora felt her cheeks flame again.

"Oh, well. The birds needed something to eat, too." Mary said over her shoulder as she led Kaaren and Knute from the room.

Ingeborge chuckled. Nora bit her lip. John grinned from one woman to the other, his eyebrow arched above his right eye. Laughter filled the room and bounced off the darkened windows.

Just like home, Nora thought. *Oh, how I've missed the laughter.*

Ingeborge settled herself in the rocker and started to nurse the baby. She flipped the baby's quilt over her shoulder and set the chair rocking.

John pulled out a chair and, after sitting down and bouncing James on his knee, reached across the table for another cookie. "How good to come home to such a happy place." He took a bite of cookie and closed his eyes in bliss. "Now, if only I had a cup of coffee to wash this down." He looked his young son in the eye, as if asking his opinion. "Wouldn't that be about right?"

Nora leaped to grab a cup and fill it to the brim. If she wanted to hire out as a housekeeper or helper, she had better begin to anticipate what a man arriving home would want.

"I hope that is hot enough." She placed it in front of him. She watched him with anxious eyes as he sipped then nodded. "Good. Now I start the dumplings."

On her way back across the kitchen she stopped to check the fire and added more coal. After moving the cooking pot to the hotter part of the stove, she raised the cover and gave the contents a stir with the wooden spoon that rested in a saucer on the warming oven.

While she mixed and stirred the dumplings, Nora listened to the conversation between the pastor and his wife. Thanks to Ingeborge's delightful descriptions, she recognized many of the people John talked about. The conclusion of both doctor and pastor: No one was available to nurse this new baby. Also, they had not talked to people about hiring Nora.

"Maybe tomorrow, after the funerals, I'll have a better idea for you," Reverend Moen told Nora. "In the meantime, we are grateful to have you here."

"Especially since all I seem to be doing is feeding babies." Ingeborge lifted baby Peder to her shoulder and patted his back.

Nora took her bowl to the stove and, after raising the lid of the steaming kettle, plopped the spoonfuls of dough onto the bubbling chicken. "There now." She resisted the habit to taste her cooking and set the kettle farther back on the range so it would simmer.

That evening, after a dinner lightened with laughter, the family remained gathered around the table for the father to read from the Bible and lead family prayers. Nora relaxed against the back of her chair, caught up in the rhythm and beauty of the Beatitudes.

"Blessed are they. . . ." The words rolled off Reverend Moen's tongue and brought a lump to

Nora's throat. It was so easy to picture herself back home and pretend this was her father reading. "Blessed" was one of her mother's favorite words.

Nora opened her eyes to lock herself into the present. These people—this family—was indeed the merciful. To take her in as they had and make her feel so much a part of them. "Thank you" hardly seemed sufficient for all the gratitude she felt.

When he prayed for Carl Detschman, she joined her thoughts and prayers with his. And for little Peder, sleeping so soundly and blissfully in the cradle at their feet. Kaaren nodded on her lap, as did Grace on Ingeborge's. But, when the "Amen" came, all the little ones joined right in.

"I'm going to take Peder to bed with me so we can keep him warm enough. Nora, I'm sorry to ask this but, will there be room for Kaaren with you and Mary? Grace is still using the crib and I dislike making a pallet on the floor in case she throws off her covers."

Nora hugged the little one on her lap even closer. "No, that will be just fine."

"Come on, Kaaren, you get to sleep with me." Mary bounced to the floor and, grabbing the little girl's hand, dragged her up the stairs.

"Me, too," Grace wailed, trying to scramble down from her father's lap.

"All right, all right." Ingeborge threw her hands over her head. "You go on up with the others." After Grace trudged part way up the stairs, Ingeborge whispered. "We'll bring her down to her crib after they all fall asleep." She gave Knute an extra hug and sent him up after the others, to his room across the hall. "I'll be up in a bit for prayers."

Nora rose to her feet and began clearing the table. "Maybe I should have Mary teach me English," she said as she stacked the plates. "She switches between English and Norwegian like she's speaking one language. I know the Bible says not to envy but I wish I knew two languages like that." She carried the dishes to the sink.

"Yah, and Kaaren speaks some German since her mother and father speak both languages. These little ones learn quickly." Ingeborge dipped water from the reservoir to fill her dishpan. "Tomorrow, we'll all begin teaching Nora English. You'll help too, won't you John?"

Reverend Moen looked up from his Bible and the papers beside it. "I'll be happy to, after the two funerals." He rubbed his forehead with the fingers of one hand. "So many we are losing. And this isn't even what you'd call a bad year."

"Did you talk with Carl again today?" Ingeborge crossed the room to rub her husband's neck and shoulders.

"No. I asked Einer, who works down at the feedstore if he could go out and let Carl's neighbors know he needed help." He leaned his head forward. "That feels so good."

Nora took Ingeborge's place at the sink and continued with the dishes. She bit her tongue against asking if she should go out and help Carl. When he came for the children, that would be the right time.

After they had shuffled all the sleeping children

into the right beds, Nora studied the faces of the two girls sleeping together. Kaaren's hair was darker, more like honey than towhead white like Mary's. Freckles dotted Kaaren's turned-up nose and the trace of a tear still lingered on one pale cheek.

Poor little lamb, Nora thought as she lifted the covers and slipped into the bed. So young to be left without a mother. No wonder she cried herself to sleep. Nora snuggled down into the featherbed and tucked the quilt around her shoulders so no cold air could sneak in.

How long would it take her to earn passage home to Norway? Could she be there by Midsummer's Eve? At home she shared the bed with her sister Clara, not two little girls who looked enough alike to be sisters.

"Dear Lord," she whispered, "please let Carl Detschman hire me so I can go home soon." But her last thoughts were not of home. Instead, a tall, blond farmer walked through her dreams and the land he strode was flat.

five

By noon the next day, Nora had a headache.

"You're trying too hard." Ingeborge patted the younger woman's shoulder as she walked by. "You can't learn to speak an entire new language in one day. Even with all of us helping you."

"But I feel like . . . like as soon as I have a word locked in my head, it takes off like a lamb running from the barn up the hill after it's mother." Nora rubbed her aching head.

"Well, the table is set and dinner is all ready so why don't you sit down with a cup of coffee and close your eyes a few minutes. Both babies are sleeping and I'll read a story to the others in the parlor." Ingeborge suited actions to her words and left Nora sitting in the rocker in front of the stove.

Nora tipped her head forward, stretching the muscles as far as she could, then leaned it back against the rocker. With one foot she set the chair in motion. The hum of the fire and the creaking-rocker song were as soothing as a cold compress on her forehead.

The fragrance of bread, fresh from the oven, and the stew simmering on the stove, mingled with the bite of the lye soap with which they had washed diapers. Strung on a line behind the stove to dry, the diapers added their own peculiar odor.

The cat meowed at her feet then leaped up in her

lap and arched it's back against the palm of her hand before circling three times to find it's comfort spot. As Nora stroked it's back, the cat's rumbling purr added harmony in bass to the kitchen quartet.

The drumbeat of her headache left her temples and escaped up the chimney pipe.

After several minutes of comfort, she heard boots scraping snow off on the step, then a fist knocking on the door. Nora swept the cat to the floor and rose to answer the summons.

Up close like this, Nora realized how tall Carl Detschman really stood. Even with the difference of the porch and house floors, he towered over her by nearly a head. Tongue-tied because she could not speak his language, Nora just stepped back and motioned him to enter.

At his "*Guten tag*," Nora bobbed her head. She was amazed. It sounded so much like Norwegian. Would they really be able to communicate?

"Come in, come in." Ingeborge and the children joined them at the door.

"Pa!" Kaaren threw herself into her father's waiting arms. She locked both arms around his neck as if defying anyone to try to remove her.

Carl Detschman stood and took off his hat but refused to venture farther into the room. He pointed to his snowy boots and shook his head. "Is Reverend Moen here?"

"Any minute now," Ingeborge shooshed the other children back. "He had another funeral this morning and then a call to make. How may I help you?"

"I . . . that is, Anna. . . ."

"Ma? I want my ma!" Kaaren placed her hands on both sides of her father's face and turned him to look at her. "Please, Pa."

Nora did not need to speak English to understand what the little girl was saying—the look on Carl Detschman's face said it all.

"Can you keep her . . . them . . . until after the funeral?" Carl asked after shushing his daughter.

"Of course. We'll talk more then. But why don't you come in and sit down to wait for Reverend Moen? What will you—"

"I can't." He drew himself straight, hugged his daughter, whispered in her ear, and handed her to Ingeborge. "I just can't." He turned and yanked open the door, the cold draft sending the women's skirts back against their legs.

The look on his face imprinted itself on Nora's mind. *Lost and angry. What a heavy burden,* she thought.

"Why didn't they have both funerals this morning?" Nora asked after they had settled the children again. Kaaren sniffed back tears once in a while—and hiccuped.

"Because Carl and Anna are German," Ingeborge snapped, "and some people in this town are hateful." She hid her mouth with the back of her fist. "Forgive me, I didn't—I shouldn't even think such things. But, much as Reverend Moen preaches to love thy neighbor, some people think that doesn't include anyone who isn't Norwegian." She shook her head. "Sometimes, being the pastor's wife isn't easy, let alone being the pastor."

"So, will anyone come to mourn with him?"

"Yah, a few."

"Why don't you go and I'll stay here with the children? Just being with you is a comfort and I know he needs that."

"Yah, that is a good idea. Thank you." Ingeborge used the edge of her apron to wipe something from the corner of her eye. "I should have fed Peder by then and I won't be gone long if James wakes up. Now I know how difficult it would be to feed twins."

Everyone ate dinner with serious faces and little talking.

"Mary, you help Miss Johanson with the dishes," Ingeborge reminded her daughter as they all rose from the table. "We won't be gone very long and I'm depending on you to show what a helper you can be."

"Yes, Ma."

"We'll bring Carl back for coffee and maybe others who attend the funeral. So would you please set out the coffee and cookies?" Ingeborge pressed a forefinger against her lips. "I have some *søtsuppe* in the pie safe also. You could bring that in and thaw it out over the stove. That, warmed, will taste good."

"Oh, I haven't had that for so long." Nora continued to clear the table. "My mother uses all kinds of fruit in hers."

"And we have cream to pour on top." Ingeborge lifted her black wool coat from the wooden coat tree and pinned on her black veiled hat while standing in

front of the mirror. "Now, you children be good for
Miss Johanson." She bent and kissed each one, including Kaaren. Then, waving her fingers, she went
out the door.

When Kaaren started to fill up with tears again,
Nora lifted the little girl in her arms and spun her
around. Laughing together, they all trooped into the
kitchen. She handed each of the children a dish
towel and as she washed each dish and cup, she
handed them, one at a time, to each child. Mary led
the game of naming every item in English with Nora
repeating the word each time. After the dishes were
done, they continued the game by naming things
around the room. When Nora forgot the word for
table, they chorused it together; when she remembered stove and oven, they cheered.

After setting the table again and finishing the
preparations for company, Nora sank down into the
chair and, lifting Grace to one knee and Kaaren to
the other, gathered Mary and Knute as close as she
could. Øye was eye and øyebryn, eyebrow. The
game continued just like teaching a baby he had a
nose and mouth.

They were all laughing over nothing when the
door opened with a blast of cold air.

"But you must have some help," Reverend Moen
was saying as they stamped snow off their feet and
entered the house. "You can't take care of all your
livestock and the children, too. How will you manage?"

"I don't know. I. . . ."

"Here, now. See how nicely Nora has prepared

things for us. Let's just sit down to eat and talk things over." Ingeborge helped the younger man off with his coat and hung it up with her own. "You can't go off without something warm in your belly."

Nora flew to set the coffeepot on the table and dish up the *søtsuppe*. Mary carried the cream pitcher and set it in front of her father.

"Pa! " Kaaren attached herself like a limpet to her father's leg.

"Is no one else coming?" Nora asked Ingeborge in a voice only they could hear.

Ingeborge shook her head. "It was getting late and they needed to get home before dark."

Nora finished the comment in her mind. Or so they said, whoever "they" were.

"Why don't you leave the children here for a few more days," Reverend Moen suggested after everyone was served. "Peder is getting stronger but we haven't found a wet nurse for him, yet. And Kaaren is doing fine here. What do you say, son?"

Carl glanced over at Ingeborge, as if asking her permission.

"Yah," she said with a nod. "I feel that is best, too."

"I appreciate what you are doing but I—"

"No buts, then. It is settled." John clapped a hand on Carl's shoulder.

Nora refilled the coffee cups and wished she knew for sure what they were saying. In a moment of silence, she took all of her courage in hand and announced, "I could go out to help Mr. Detschman with the house and the children. If we get Peder to take a bottle, there wouldn't be any problem." She stopped to look at the Moens' faces, took a deep breath and continued. "You said there wasn't anyone else and . . . and this way I could earn my passage money back home . . . to Norway . . . that is . . . if Mr. Detschman can afford . . . ah. . . ." This time she could not pick up the words again.

"Certainly not!" Reverend Moen shook his head. "Why he couldn't—you couldn't—"

"What he means to say is that you're not married," Ingeborge interposed softly, "and if you, as an unmarried woman, went out to work for Carl, your reputation would be ruined. No one would ever marry you."

"But . . . but. . . ."

"Thank you, Miss Johanson." Carl answered after Reverend Moen translated the conversation for him. "But they are correct."

Nora tried to remember the good reasons she had thought of earlier but, in the face of their unified disapproval, she fell silent. She had thought things might be different here in the new country but the old customs still held sway.

"I just thought this might be a way out of a difficult situation for both of us." She raised her chin and sat up even straighter. "I need work and you need a worker." She thought she saw a ghost of a smile soften his mouth and eyes but she must have been mistaken—when she looked again, the glacier had taken over his eyes and voice.

"I thank you for all your kindnesses. I'll return on Sunday for church and to pick up the children, if that will be all right." Carl whispered in his daughter's ear and set Kaaren down on her feet. When she clung to him, he gently disengaged her fingers. "I'll see you on Sunday and then we'll go home," he promised.

"Thank you again, Miss Johanson." He nodded in her direction and, after shaking hands and thanking the others, he shrugged into his wool coat and bent over to plant a kiss on his daughter's wet cheek. "You be a big girl now."

"Pa!" The forlorn child leaned her head against the door after it closed after him. "Ma-a-a. I want Ma."

Ingeborge scooped the whimpering child up into her arms. "Your ma has gone to live with Jesus in heaven, little one." She kissed away the tears and crooned soft words until Kaaren quit crying.

He never even looked at the baby, Nora thought as she and Mary cleared the table. And I still think mine was a good idea.

Up in her room that night, before falling to sleep, Nora carefully penned a letter to her family. When she told them about Hans's passing away, she did not mention the lies. She described the trip and the Moens. And said she would be looking for work.

She fell asleep thinking of eyes the blue of a glacier ice cave, shimmering in the sun. But the eyes were so sad as to bring tears to her own.

Saturday, the entire house had to be cleaned and the food prepared for Sunday. Nora and Ingeborge worked with a rhythm that showed how close they had become. The naming game continued with new words thrown in to make sentences.

"This is a table." Nora said as she waxed the shiny surface. Kaaren and Mary clapped their hands. "This is a chair." Big smiles. "This is a. . . ." Nora raised her hands in the air and shrugged.

"Rug," the girls chimed. "This is a rug."

"And it needs to be shaken. Take it out on the back porch." Ingeborge told her daughter. The two little girls picked up the corners and carried the woven rag rug out the back. "And shake it good."

Late in the afternoon, Ingeborge sat nursing baby Peder and Nora had the children gathered around her telling them a story of trolls. Even Kaaren laughed at the funny faces and voices Nora used for each character. When the story was finished, Nora hugged each of them and set the two littlest girls off her lap.

"You will make a wonderful mother," Ingeborge said after the children trooped off to play. "You are so good with the little ones. And what a help you've been to me. I'm spoiled already."

"Thank you. You make me feel like one of the family."

They rocked in companionable silence. Little Peder burped once into the stillness and continued his soft nursing noises.

"What will happen to Carl?" Nora finally asked, softly. "How will he manage?" She knew she should refer to the man as Mr. Detschman but he could only be Carl in her mind.

"I don't know." Ingeborge leaned her head against

the back of the rocker and stared up at the ceiling. "He has family in Minnesota but he doesn't think any of them can help. His sister is still too young to come out here and the others all have families of their own."

"What about a bottle for Peder?"

"We'll start him on that tonight. I wanted to give him as much breast milk as possible." She lifted the baby to her shoulder and rubbed his back. "Since he's so much stronger now, I think he'll be all right."

"Then I can feed him." Nora looked across the dimming light to her friend in the other chair.

"That you can. He'll have two bottle-feedings before we go to bed and then I'll nurse him in the middle of the night." She chuckled softly. "God certainly knew what He was doing when He created mothers and babies. This one is such a love." She nestled him back into the crook of her arm and trailed a finger across the baby's closed fist. Her sigh seemed to come from deep within her heart. "I love babies so." She kissed the baby's cheek and looked up. "Here, you hold him for a while and I'll get the supper going."

Nora accepted the bundled infant and settled him into her arms, like Ingeborge had done in her arms. She watched the baby's eyelids flutter and the perfect little mouth pucker and relax. "He is so beautiful." How could one do anything but whisper in the face of such a miracle?

Several hours later, she felt the same awe but only more so when she got the baby to take a bottle.

While he fussed at first, he finally sucked on the nipple and settled down to feed. Nora felt like she had climbed the highest mountain near the farm at home.

Sometime later, in the middle of the darkest night, Nora awoke to the sniffling and tears of Kaaren, crying for her mother. Nora gathered the sobbing child into her arms. With hands of love, she brushed the straggles of hair from Kaaren's face and wiped away the tears.

"I . . . uh . . . want . . . my . . . ma. Why doesn't she come?"

Nora murmured responses in her own language, wishing she could say the things in her heart to this grieving child. Ingeborge had told her that her mother had gone to be with Jesus. That she was not coming back. But how could such a little one understand that?

Softly, so she would not wake Mary, Nora began to sing. "Jesus loves me. . . ." As the words and love in the song crept into that silent night, she felt the child relax against her shoulder. Jerky, leftover sobs that wracked the small body tore at Nora's heart. "Yes, Jesus loves me. . . ." She finished the song on a whisper and removed her arm from under Kaaren's neck.

"Heavenly Father, comfort this family," she prayed. "Bring back the love they've lost and, if You want me to care for them, please find a way. Amen."

Forgotten were the tears of the night as the two

girls bounced up to greet the sun sparkling around the feathery frost patterns on the windowpane. They ran, giggling down the stairs, leaving Nora to stretch and twist her body from one side to the other in the softness of the deep feather ticking. When she heard a baby crying, she leaped from the bed, put on her wrapper and made her way downstairs.

Ingeborge was jostling James on her hip while warming a bottle for Peder who was crying in Mary's arms in the rocker.

"And a good morning to you, too," Nora said with a laugh while relieving Mary of her squalling bundle.

"Good. Now I can take care of this one," Ingeborge sank gratefully into the other rocker. "He thinks his mother should drop everything the minute he cries. What a spoiled little boy."

Nora tested the warmth of the bottled milk on one of her wrists and then sat down to begin the feeding. Peder fussed a bit, not quite willing to take the bottle. "Come now. We did this beautifully last night. Ingeborge isn't going to be here to feed you anymore."

Peder looked up at her as if he understood every word she had said. When she prodded his closed lips with the nipple again, he took it and began to suck like she might take it away before he could fill himself.

Nora chuckled. What a precious baby. And smart, too, she could already tell.

"Mary, you set the table. We'll have mush as soon as I finish here so put the cinnamon and cream on the table."

"Where's Pa?" Mary asked as she handed the bowls, one at a time to Grace and Kaaren.

"Starting the furnace at the church. Then, he's planning to work more on his sermon. I told him it was too cold over there and that he should come home to finish."

"And?" Nora set the chair rocking.

"And he's over there in the cold because he says he can't work with all the noise around here." Inge's glance around the kitchen included the chattering children as all four went about their chores, Mary firmly telling each one what to do. The teakettle sang merrily on the stove and, up until a few minutes ago, there had been two babies crying. "I just don't understand why he thinks this is noisy." Her eyebrows nearly met her hairline.

Nora laughed along with her friend. "This is the way homes are supposed to be. Someday, I want one just like this." She put the baby up to her shoulder and patted his back. "Just like this."

"With two babies at a time?"

"Well. . . .Maybe one by one."

The clock bonged eight times.

"We must hurry if we don't want to be late to Sunday School. Here, Mary, you take James while I finish making the breakfast. The table looks lovely."

While she was giving out assignments, Reverend Moen let in a blast of cold air as he came through the door. "What a beautiful day we have," he said as he hung up his coat and hat. "Why it's ten degrees above zero and getting warmer. Pretty soon, the Chinook will come sighing across the plains and, before you know it, spring will be here."

He rubbed his hands together, warming them above the stove. "Wait until you see spring here on the prairie, Nora. It is like no other season."

Nora, like a good guest, kept her doubts to herself. What could possibly be beautiful about this flat country? Now, spring in Norway—that was sight and sound to behold. The cracking thunder as the rivers broke loose from their winter dungeon and the logs cascaded down with the ice floes. The birds returning in flocks to darken the sky and the masses of green bursting forth from the soil as the sun shone longer each day.

The ache of homesickness caught her by surprise. To stem any tears that threatened to overflow, she swallowed the lump in her throat and rolled her eyes upward. Better remember that Old Man Winter still held her beloved homeland in his icy grip.

"I . . . I'll take Peder with me while I go get ready. Unless you need me for something else first?"

"No, no. You go on." Ingeborge shooshed her away with fluttering hands. She went back to stirring the mush that was thickening under her watchful eye.

"I'll hurry." With the baby in one arm and the pitcher of warm water from the reservoir in the other, Nora went up the stairs. She propped the infant against the pillows and continued talking with him as she washed her face and hands. Before she was half done, he had fallen off to sleep.

With Reverend Moen encouraging haste, they finished eating and cleaning up in time to be bundled up and out the door and arriving at the church as the first of the other families were hitching their horses to the rails.

It felt like home to Nora and yet she felt strange and out of place. This was the first time in her life she had worshipped in a church other than the one at home. While people were speaking Norwegian around her, none of them were her relatives. At home her aunts and uncles and cousins, besides brothers and sisters made up half of the congregation.

Nora smiled as each person was introduced. But she kept waiting for one man, Carl Detschman, to appear. He had said he would join them for church but he still had not arrived as the organist played the opening songs.

They had settled in the front pew. Nora rocked the baby in her arms, Kaaren was beside her, and Mary next. Ingeborge was shushing Grace and Knute. What a pewful they made.

Nora did not realize until the closing hymn how much she had been waiting for a tall, broad-shouldered farmer to join their group. She kept hoping he had sat in the back and, when they turned to leave, she thought she saw that familiar blond head leaving before anyone else. He had said he would join them for church. If it was him, why did he leave so quickly?

Peder had slept through the service, much to Nora's relief, but, when they stood for the benediction, he began whimpering. By the time she could get out the door, he had progressed into the demanding stage.

"I'll take him home and feed him," Nora whispered to Ingeborge as she passed the Moens in the greeting line at the front door. At the top of the three wooden stairs, Nora stopped for a moment to look again for Carl Detschman. Was that Carl driving his sleigh down the street?

"Don't be silly," she scolded herself on the short walk back to the parsonage. "It doesn't matter one whit to you if the man came to church or not. Once he picks up his children, you probably won't even see him again. Ingeborge said he was unpopular—an outcast—because of his German heritage. So just put a smile on your face and enjoy the day. You won't have to worry about whether this darling bundle of baby eats or not. It's his father's problem."

So, then, why did her bottom lip feel like it wanted to quiver? And what was that stupid lump in her throat? How could she let these babies go without someone there to take care of them?

She hurried through the door of the parsonage and slammed it shut behind her. In the time it took her to warm the bottle and settle down to feed the crying infant, the remainder of the family arrived home. They were chattering and laughing about their chores when a knock sounded at the door.

"Welcome, Carl." Reverend Moen ushered the visitor in. "I was happy to see you come to the service. Let me take your coat and hat."

"Thank you."

Kaaren made her usual beeline for her father's legs.

"Dinner is almost ready," Ingeborge said while bending down to remove the roast from the oven. "You're just in time."

Nora clutched little Peder tighter. *How had she gotten so attached to these two children in such a short time?*

"Miss Johanson, Reverend, Missus, can we talk for a few minutes? Right away?" Carl ducked his chin, then squared his shoulders. "Please?"

Ingeborge wiped her hands on the dish towel she had slung over her shoulder. "Of course. Mary, you take the children into the other room to play. Nora, Peder can go back in the cradle now. "

Nora shook her head. She could not lay the baby down, not when he was to be taken away from her so soon. "I . . . I'll just rock him. He was fussing a moment ago."

"No—I mean, please could you join us?" Carl motioned to a chair at the table.

Nora stood and, after laying Peder in the cradle as asked, walked to the table and sank down on one of the oak chairs. With the tip of her finger, she smoothed a spot on the table. Something strange was happening here.

"Miss Johanson, Nora, would you marry me?"

six

Nora felt her chin drop—clear to her chest.

"I know this is sudden, but let me tell you what I am thinking. As the Moens said, you cannot come live at my farm without marriage. It would not be proper. But, if we were married, your living there and caring for my children would be all right. I will advertise for a housekeeper in the Fargo and Grand Forks papers and, when we find one, then we will have the marriage annulled and I will pay for your passage to return to Norway."

He waited while Ingeborge finished translating.

I can go home to Norway, was Nora's first thought. *I would have a place to work*, was her second, and *I won't have to give up these babies*, was the third. *At least not for a time*, she amended. She closed her eyes, the better to think. *But marriage! An annulment?*

Her gaze flew to Reverend Moen's face. "Will this work?"

John rubbed his nose with the index finger of his right hand. "A marriage can be annulled only if it is not consummated."

Nora felt her cheeks flame at the thought. Surely Mr. Detschman understood that . . . that they would not share a bed.

"You and the children will share the big bedroom downstairs, where it is warm. I will fix a bed for me

83

upstairs." Carl ducked his chin and stammered over the last words. "I mean, this marriage would be because . . . to . . . ah . . . save your reputation." His voice deepened to a growl. "That is all I have to offer."

Nora nodded that she understood. And what he was offering was enough for her. Since Hans had lied and died, she wanted nothing to do with North Dakota farmers. She would dream of returning home. This seemed to be a sensible solution.

"What do you think, Ingeborge?" Nora risked looking at her friend.

"I don't know." She looked from her husband to the man still standing, his hand now resting on the back of a chair. "You and the children can stay here for as long as you need."

When Carl understood her response, he shook his head. "I cannot lay such a burden upon you. You have already been good to me beyond duty."

"Let us eat our dinner and think about this plan of yours," Reverend Moen said. "You have not proposed an easy thing."

Nora let the conversation at dinner flow around her like a river around a big rock. It wasn't that she did not understand half of it, she just needed the time to think.

What would her mother say? Surely I would be home almost before they could send a reply. All I need tell them is that I am caring for two small children for a farmer here who lost his wife. An annulment is like the marriage had never been.

And I can go home soon. Back to the mountains,

with green forests and white rushing rivers. Back to
my family . . . Clara and Einer, Gunhilde and
Thorliff. And little Sophie—she won't be all grown
up before I see her again. She pictured each of them
in her mind.

Halfway through the meal, Peder began his waking whimpers. By the time Nora had a bottle
warmed, he had progressed to red-faced demand.

Nora picked him up and whisked him off for a
diaper change. Then, she took her place in the
rocker and silenced him with the nipple. As the baby
sucked, she let her mind roam back across the ocean
again. But it refused to stay in Norway.

Instead, she thought of the baby in her arms. If she
did not stay, who would care for him? And little
Kaaren. She was still waking at night, calling for
her mother. Would her father be able to care for her
. . . and do all his farming, too? Spring planting
would come and then how would he manage?

Her mind flitted to the man himself. He is so
stern. Was this his usual way or was it due to his
great sorrow? His children needed some love and
light in their lives.

Of course, he could leave them with the Moens,
like Ingeborge had suggested, but what if Nora went
to work somewhere else? How could Ingeborge
handle her home and all the children by herself?

After letting her thoughts race like a fox after
rabbits, she tipped her head back. *Father God, what
would You have me to do?* Her thoughts quit their
scampering. She had prayed earlier for Him to work
something out, hadn't she? Was this it?

When Peder finished eating, she rose and walked back to the table. "Yah, I will do this." She nodded as she spoke. "Carl Detschman, I will marry you."

"Today?"

She stared at him. Had she understood? She looked to Ingeborge for confirmation.

"I don't see what the rush is," Reverend Moen said, shaking his head. "Next week—"

"No. If we are going to do this, we will do this now." Carl kept his gaze on Nora's face.

Nora took a deep breath and let it out, along with all her hesitations. "Now."

"Let me warm up the church first." Reverend Moen rose to his feet and reached for his coat.

"No!" Nora cried then repeated more softly. "No, we'll be married in the parlor, not the church. Since this wedding doesn't count anyway, I do not want the ceremony to be performed in the church."

"If you are certain." John hung his coat back up.

Nora nodded. She kept her gaze on the part in Kaaren's hair. She could not look up at Carl, not right now.

Although the ceremony was spoken in Norwegian, Nora heard the words with only the top part of her mind. The rest of her floated in a fog. She gave the proper answers when Reverend Moen asked her to but she never looked above the Bible clasped in his hands.

"I have no ring," Carl said, as he held Nora's hand. "But if you like, I will buy one the next time I come into town."

"No. That is not necessary." Why was there a

lump in her throat? After all, this ceremony meant nothing. They really were not married—were they?

Carl and Reverend Moen loaded Nora's trunk into the wagon while the women gathered up all the children's things. Nora repacked her carpetbag and carried it downstairs to the front door.

"I can't believe this is happening." Ingeborge took Nora's cold hands in hers and held them together. "If you need anything, remember your big sister is always here to help you."

Nora tried to smile around the quiver in her chin—Ingeborge was anything but big. Leaving here was almost as hard as leaving home.

The women wrapped Peder in his blankets and then an extra quilt before following the men out the door. Carl had spread hay in the back of the wagon and, with extra quilts, made a nest for his family. Nora placed her hand in his and, using the runners for a step, joined Kaaren in the box. Ingeborge handed Peder in to her.

Carl swung up to the high board seat and unwound the reins from the whip stock. "Thank you, for everything." He tipped his hat to the Moens who stood by the side, arms around each other.

"Come and visit when you can." He clucked to the team. With a flick of the reins, the horses started forward, the iron sled runners creaking in the snow.

The goodbyes rang on the clear air. Nora waved from her shelter. Kaaren waved one last time, then snuggled down into the warm nest of quilts. She leaned her head against Nora's arm and, tipping up her face, smiled broader than Nora had yet seen.

The smile sent angels of joy dancing in Nora's heart. Surely she had made the right choice. She smiled back, then tucked the quilts more closely about them with her free hand. With the sun on it's downward slide, the temperature was already dropping. She edged the long scarf draped around her neck up and over the hat she had pinned so securely in place. Hats like hers may be fashionable but they were not worth anything in a snowstorm.

Carl hunkered down in his seat, offering little of himself to the wind. He flicked the reins again, bringing the team up to a smart trot. The way the sun was sinking, they would barely be home just before dark. He had not planned on spending so much time at the Moens'.

Oh Anna, he cried in the confines of his heart, *have I done the right thing? Little Kaaren needs you so desperately and so do I. The house is empty without you. I'd rather sleep in the barn where at least there is some noise with the animals.*

He covered his nose with the red scarf wrapped around his neck. "Come on, boys. Let's get home." The harness jingled soprano while the hooves thudded bass. The runners creaked in counterpoint but the symphony was lost on the man hunkered on the driver's seat. He wandered in a frozen, desolate land where music and laughter were outlawed.

How would he talk with this woman he was bringing home? Granted, he had learned some Norwegian since coming to Soldall and Norwegian and German had some similarities, but she had to learn English—he would insist. His daughter would grow up speaking English—no people would laugh behind her back. He remembered the cruelty of children, especially at school.

He shivered against the cold. But the cold within him was deeper than weather could bring.

Nora, snuggled down in the bed of the wagon, now turned sleigh, was nearly asleep when a halt jerked her upright. A dog leaped and barked beside them. They were stopped in front of a square, two-storied house, the kind that dotted the prairie like toys tossed out by a giant hand. A snowdrift reached like a dragging scarf clear up to one second-story window. She craned her neck around the rumps of the steaming horses to see the red hip-roofed barn, silo, and other outbuildings. A tingle ran up her spine. Mr. Detschman owned a fine farm.

Kaaren stirred from her sound asleep. "Are we home, Pa?"

"Yes, little one, we are." He leaned over the edge of the box and lifted his little girl out. "Here." He handed her a parcel. "Bring this into the house."

When Nora held out the quilt-wrapped baby to him, he took her arm instead and steadied her as she clambered down to the shoveled walk to the house, the infant clutched to her chest. She would have liked to have taken a few moments to look around but dusk was on them, tinting the snow the bluish gray of eventide. She hurried up the path to open the door for Kaaren.

When she glanced back, Carl was throwing robes over the horses. He must plan on unloading my trunk right now, she thought. I should go back and help.

Peder squirmed in her arms. No, the baby came first. And it would not be long before the entire world would know that it was feeding time. Maybe the water in the stove's reservoir would still be warm enough to heat the bottle.

"Ma! Ma?" Kaaren yelled into the stillness of the empty house as soon as the door opened. "Ma, where are you?" She ran from room to room, calling, until she collapsed against the bed in the room off the kitchen. "Ma-a-a-a. I want my ma."

Nora felt like joining in the little girl's tears. How could she help this precious little one? And the baby who needed her, too—right now if his utterings were to be quieted.

Where in heaven's name was their father?

She followed Kaaren into the bedroom and laid Peder in his quilts in the middle of the bed, unwrapping him only enough to allow him to breathe easily. Then, she scooped Kaaren up in her arms, holding her tightly while she cried. While she could not speak the language, words larded with love and comfort could be felt by anyone. *Could she be the mother they needed?*

When Kaaren's sobs turned to sniffles, Nora set the child on the bed and, taking her hand, patted Peder's chest. "You do that," she said, depending on sign language. "Be good to your brother. Good, good." She nodded and smiled her approval as Kaaren gently continued the patting. "Keep on, more." Nora backed from the room, all the while smiling and nodding, and headed for the stove.

The reservoir water was still plenty warm so Nora searched through the lower cupboards to find a small pan. She filled it half-full with water, then went back into the bedroom for one of the baby's bottles of milk she had brought from Ingeborge's.

Nora could tell Peder was tired of being patted. His whimper had turned to a howl so she picked him up. While rocking him in her one arm, she set the bottle into the warm water with the other hand.

"I do not know how all those women managed with just one arm for so many years," she muttered as she continued to lift the stove lid, add coal, replace the lid, open the damper and comfort the hungry baby. "Your supper will be ready soon. Shhhhh." She swayed with the soothing rhythm that has been passed down through the centuries from woman to woman.

Kaaren wandered into the kitchen and hid her face in Nora's skirt, clinging to the fabric as if that, too, might be taken from her. Nora patted the little girl's hair with her free hand.

Where was their father?

With the baby finally nursing contentedly in her arm, Nora relaxed in the rocking chair. Kaaren stuck to her side like a barnacle on a rock. I suppose I should make supper, Nora thought as she rocked, but what? You would think Carl would be here to show me where things are. That would be the decent thing to do.

She looked around the room. We could eat eggs if he has chickens. Is there any bread? Even toast and hot milk would be enough, at least for Kaaren and me. She studied the white painted cupboards, the sink with a bucket below to catch the water. A red, long-handled pump was bolted to the outer edge. How wonderful, to have water piped into the house.

Lace curtains with red tiebacks brightened every window, both the smaller one above the sink and the double-sashed one on the other side of the round oak table. As in all homes, the large black, cast-iron stove took up much of the space.

If the remainder of the house was as comfortable as the kitchen, Nora thought, I'll love working here. And soon, I'll be able to take the ship back to Norway.

With the baby fed, burped, changed, and put to bed in the cradle by the bed in the other room, Nora picked up the kerosene lamp she had lit, took Kaaren by the hand, and went exploring. The parlor, with both doors closed, was freezing, as was Kaaren's small bedroom in the back of the house. The little girl picked up a rag doll, hugging it to her.

"Come along, let's go back to the kitchen where it is warm."

To keep from wasting the heat, Nora closed all the doors behind them. Back in the kitchen, she found a door in the stair wall with a well-stocked pantry on one side and stairs down to the cellar on the other.

Kaaren stood in the doorway, one finger in her mouth and dragging the doll with her other hand. But she never took her gaze off the woman opening drawers and doors.

"Bread, good." Nora nodded as she talked to herself. "Jam." She gathered the items in her arms. "Butter." She opened a door on the end wall that was screened to the outside. "Ah, milk. But it's frozen." She handed the bread to Kaaren. "You carry this." Then she picked up the jug of milk. "Supper will be coming soon."

She set the milk to thawing in a pan of water on the stove while she sliced bread and set it in the toaster racks she had found hanging on the back of the warming oven. Then, opening the lid on the stove, she laid the rack over the burning coals. By the time the bread was browned, Nora felt toasted as well.

With the milk that had thawed and some toast with jam, Nora and Kaaren set themselves in the rocking chair and started to eat. Nora began the game. "This is . . . ?" She pointed at the bread.

"Bread. This is bread." Kaaren nodded and took a bite.

Nora pointed to the rich, red jam. "This is . . . ?"

"Jam." They grinned at each other as they chewed and swallowed.

First, they named the milk, the cup, the plate, and each time, Nora repeated the sentence. When they were finished eating, they remained in the chair, rocking slowly. Nora began humming a song her mother used to sing. When she was humming she did not have to think about Carl Detschman or to where he had so rudely disappeared. If he was out doing chores, as was most likely, he could have come in the house first and showed her where things were kept. Kaaren settled back against Nora's chest and soon closed her eyes. Before long, the small body slumped in sleep.

Nora had almost drowsed off when the thud of boots, kicking off the snow against the steps on the porch, startled her awake. She started to get up then thought the better of it. If Carl Detschman wanted any supper beyond bread and milk this night, he would just have to sing for it.

seven

Peder demanded to be fed every two hours—all night, and all the next day. By the third morning, Nora felt like she had been trampled by six hitch teams of horses. If Carl had heard the baby crying, either night or day, he ignored it. That might be possible at night since he was sleeping upstairs but, during the day? Granted, he was never in the house except for meals but. . . .

The day before, Nora had passed the disgusted stage and now she was bordering on anger—if only she had the strength to even spark. She leaned her head against the door of the cupboard. Kneading bread took more power than she had thought—anything took more energy than she could summon.

Right now, the baby was sleeping. If she could only get Kaaren down for a nap, then she could sleep, too.

The thought of sleep nearly overwhelmed her. "But first you must finish the bread." Lately, she had found herself talking to herself more often than not.

She and Kaaren still played the naming game but it was not the same as having a real, live, grown-up to talk with. Mr. Carl Detschman though, spoke only in grunts and language between them was not a barrier—there just wasn't any. How would she ever learn enough English this way?

She slammed the dough over on the floured surface and pressed it hard with the heel of her hand. Roll the dough in, press and turn, roll the dough in, press and turn. The rhythm continued.

At night, the temperature would fall to well below zero so she kept both Kaaren and Peder in bed with her to keep them warm enough. During her nocturnal feeding forays, she would dream of warmer weather and how nice it would be if she could sleep straight through to spring.

She thumped the bread one last time, molded it into a round, and poked the dough with her finger. When the dough sprang back, she placed it into an earthenware bowl, covered it with a dish towel, and set the bowl on the warming oven to rise. After stirring the beans that were baking in the oven, she removed her apron and slung it over a chair.

"Come, Kaaren." She reached over to take the little girl's hand. "We're going to take a nap, you and I." She put her finger to her lips. "And we must be very quiet so Peder can sleep longer, too."

Kaaren put her finger to her lips and silently climbed up onto the bed. She scooted over to the other side, then sat on her knees. "Sing?"

Nora shook her head. "Sleep." She lifted the quilt and motioned to Kaaren to get under it. Kaaren flung herself back onto the pillow and lifted her feet, shoes still buttoned on, into the air.

"This is a shoe." Her eyes sparkled with anticipation.

"No. Sleep, not play."

Kaaren spoke more insistently. "This is a shoe."

Nora put her finger to her lips. "Shhhh. Yah, this

is a shoe but now we sleep." She snuggled down and tucked the quilt around their shoulders.

Kaaren lay flat on the pillow, her eyes wide open. *Please little one*, Nora pleaded silently, *go to sleep. I am so tired my eyes won't stay open.* Under her breath she began to hum a song her mother used to sing.

Nora felt the warmth of the quilt steal over her. The little body next to her relaxed, along with hers. Her hum grew jerky until it faded away to nothing.

Somewhere in another world she heard a door close.

"Pa!" Kaaren flew out from under the covers and slid to the floor. "Pa!" Screaming voice, thundering feet.

Peder set up his own welcome, also at the top of his lungs.

Nora lay there with her eyes closed. Maybe Peder would go back to sleep. Maybe Carl would take his lively daughter outside with him for a while. Maybe. She was too tired for any more maybes.

She pushed back the quilt and swung her feet over the side of the bed. Head in her hands, she waited for Peder to settle down again but his demands grew louder.

"I'm coming." She slid her feet into her carpet slippers, pulled herself to her feet, and walked over to the cradle to pick up the hungry baby. With the baby in one arm, and pushing a strand of hair back into her braids with the other hand, she entered the kitchen to find Carl pouring himself a cup of coffee.

"I'm going into Soldall," he said in German,

slowly so she could understand. "Don't worry about the cows if I return after dark. I'll be as quick as I can."

"I go, Pa? Please?" Kaaren wrapped both her arms around his leg, her face raised in supplication.

"No." He shook his head. "It's too cold outside for a little girl like you."

Nora stopped her bottle preparations and turned to look at him. He had spoken more words in the last two minutes than he had done in the last three days.

As he made his way to the door, Kaaren still clung to him. "Now, be a good girl. You can watch out the window." He stood her on the chair so she could see out.

Her lower lip quivered. A tear stood like a bead at the edge of one brilliant, blue eye. "Pa-a-a." The one word held all the woe of a little girl left behind.

Nora dug a cookie out of the jar. "Here. Your pa will be home soon." She placed the cookie in the limp hand and caught the child in a hug. Together, they watched the driver and team trot down the lane. Peder's cries increased in volume.

After feeding the baby, Nora punched down the risen bread dough and placed it on the cupboard where it would not rise so quickly. Then, she set the boiler onto the stove to start heating some water to wash the diapers. She could barely keep up with the baby's clothes. Once the diapers were boiling merrily, she set the boiler to the cooler side of the stove and, taking Kaaren by the hand, headed back for the bed. This time, there would be no interruptions.

Kaaren scrubbed a fist across her eyes to rub out

the last of her tears and then turned onto her side and was asleep before Nora had finished settling the quilt.

"Thank you, Heavenly Father." Nora breathed the prayer as sleep claimed her.

By the time Carl returned from town, dusk had blued the snow. Nora was slicing bread when she heard the jingling of the harness. Was that joy she felt leaping in her midsection, just because the lord of the manor was home again? Well, maybe not leaping but more like stretching.

She shook her head at her silly thoughts. Her mother's words echoed for her. "Of kindness there is no equal." Calling Carl Detschman lord of the manor might not be kind, but it was true—wasn't it? The way he gave orders and without a smile—not even for his little daughter who needed love and laughter so desperately. But perhaps he had never been a smiling person. Many Norwegians were like that, too. Handsome yes, but smiling, no.

She pinched off a small piece of crust and put it into her mouth. *I wonder what it would take to make Lord Carl smile?* The thought lasted until Carl entered the house, bringing in cold air, a sack of supplies from the store, and—

"There's a letter for you." Without even looking at her, he handed her the envelope.

"*Mange takk.*" Nora's eyes devoured the handwriting—a letter from her mother. An ache in her chest made Nora press her lips together. She ignored the burning behind her eyes and tucked the beloved envelope into her apron pocket. She would save it for later, when she could read it alone. For now she must get supper on the table quickly so Carl could do his chores.

That night, after Carl had gone up to bed and the children slept, Nora poured herself a cup of coffee and sat down at the table where the light from the kerosene lamp was the strongest. With trembling fingers, she slit the envelope open and withdrew two sheets of paper.

She was almost afraid to begin reading. What if it was bad news? She shook her head and took a sip of coffee.

> *Dearest Nora,*
> *I take pen in hand to tell you how much we love you and miss you. . . .*

Nora put her head down on the table and allowed the tears to flow. The ache had grown to a roaring pain that tore at her heart and soul. How she missed those beloved faces. She could see her mother at the kitchen table, writing so carefully on the precious paper.

When she was able, Nora dried her eyes with her apron and read on. All were well. Her older brother, Einer, was courting one of the Kielguard daughters. They had all been out skiing. Father and the boys had been up in the forest cutting wood. Ice fishing had been good. How were she and Hans? Did she like North Dakota?

Nora wiped another tear from her eye. How sur-

prised they would be when her letter arrived—
shocked would be more like it. She read the letter
again and sighed. Life took strange turns and
twists—and when you least expected it.

Nora tried to catch a yawn but, instead, it nearly
dislocated her jaw. If only she could stay awake
long enough to write back. But, there was as much
chance of that as a fox turning down a juicy chicken.
She adjusted the stove damper, blew out the lamp,
and made her way into the bedroom.

Please Peder. Sleep longer. This had become her
consistent prayer and plea and tonight was no ex-
ception. She knelt at the edge of her bed and tried to
pray but even in so cramped a position, she nearly
nodded off. Nora was asleep as soon as she pulled
up the quilt around herself.

For the next week, Peder continued his demand
for being fed every two hours and sometimes he
screamed instead of sleeping between feedings.
Nothing Nora did made him content. While he was
not sick, he was not content, either.

"Hush, hush, my little one," Nora crooned one
night in the wee hours when she would have much
preferred sleep. She had tried singing to and walking the colicky baby, rubbing his back and then
trying the rocker for a time. But she had been so
tired that night she had even fallen asleep in the
rocker with him and woke up in the morning, cold
and stiff, when Carl came down the stairs to head
for milking.

"I . . . I'm sorry," she whispered as she rubbed the

sleep from her eyes.

He glanced her way but without looking into her face. With a barely perceptible nod, he turned back to the stove, added coal from the bucket, and opened the damper to bring up more heat.

She watched as he made his way out the door, looking like he carried a ten-ton load of coal on his shoulders. "*Uff da.*" She shook her head. "What will become of him?" Even she, who did not know him, could see that the light in his eyes had gone out.

Nora stiffly stood with Peder in her arms and carried him to the bedroom. Together, they went to bed and—Peder started to whimper.

By the end of the next week, Nora could concentrate only on putting one foot in front of the other. Feed the baby, prepare a meal, wash the diapers, feed the baby—when would she be able to add sleep to the routine? At the same time, Kaaren grew fussy, her temper popping out in unexpected places.

Carl had just come in the house for dinner when his daughter tripped over the edge of the rug and banged her knee. "*Uff da,*" she said with a scowl.

"Speak in English," Carl ordered over his shoulder. He turned from the sink with dripping hands. "We speak English here."

"Nora doesn't." The little girl stomped her foot.

Nora hid a grin in baby Peder's blanket. She had understood what was said that time.

"Nora?" asked Carl.

"Yah." She turned to Carl with a look that dared him to say more.

Carl changed his mind. "We'll talk later," he spoke in German, slowly.

That will be a change, Nora thought as she filled the soup bowls at the stove. When she leaned over to help Kaaren with her bread, she heard the little girl muttering very, very softly.

"*Uff da, uff da, uff da.*" Her bottom lip stuck out and her eyebrows met each other in a line that Nora knew meant trouble.

"Nora, can I speak with you in the parlor?" Carl spoke slowly and nodded to the closed room.

With his back poker-straight and his hands clenched, Carl led the way into the freezing room. "Now." He stepped around her and closed the door. "Kaaren must speak English. No Norwegian."

Nora crossed her arms across her chest. She could feel her jaw tightening. She straightened her tired back and suddenly she did not feel quite so weary. "Yah!"

"You must learn to speak English."

"Yah!" Nora shook a finger in his face as all her mother's preaching against the evils of her daughter's temper flew right up the chimney with the smoke.

"Yah! You tell me to speak English! How I would love to; if only I could! Who is there to teach me? A three-year-old who is just learning to talk?" Nora tried to slow her words down so he could understand her but it was like stopping a freight train. "I thought you would teach me—yah, you do not even talk. You don't talk to me. You don't talk to Kaaren. Maybe you talk to your cows!" With that, she spun around, yanked open the door to the kitchen, stomped through, and slammed it shut in his face.

The resounding crash woke Peder who began to wail. Kaaren stared at her, eyes wide and chin quivering.

"*Uff da!*" Nora picked up the baby and carried him off for a change of britches. She heard Carl leave, gently closing the door behind him.

She sank down onto the bed, the fury draining away as quickly as it came. What had she done?

Silence hung in the air that night at supper and Nora could feel Carl watching her. Now she knew what a mouse stalked by a cat felt like.

Every morning Nora promised herself she would write to her family. At the end of each weary day though, the letter still lived only in her mind.

One night, it seemed like she and her unhappy burden paced all night. Finally, she collapsed into the rocking chair. When she awoke, a quilt swaddled her from neck to toe. *Carl. He did this,* she thought. Warmth beyond that of the quilt seeped clear to her finger tips.

But her head ached, her nose dripped, and her eyes felt like they were glued shut. When she put Peder down in the cradle so she could begin the mush for breakfast, she started coughing.

The next morning, both Peder and Kaaren had runny noses and whiny voices. Nora coughed, Kaaren coughed, Peder coughed—and wailed.

By the next morning the baby's throat was so scratchy he could hardly cry. Nora had the kettle steaming on the stove. But, when she leaned her head over it and tried to inhale deeply, her coughing cut her off. If only she had some of her mother's special cold mixture.

The dog, barking outside, drew her to the window in time to see a horse and sleigh pulling to a stop in front of the door. Who could be calling?

Nora looked around the room. Dishes were still on the table; diapers were simmering on the stove; there was nothing in the house to serve with the coffee; her hair was not combed; the children were sick. She looked down at her dirty apron. What would they think of her?

While she took off her apron with one hand, Nora tried, with the other hand, to tuck some loose strands of hair up into her braids. She had finished neither when the knock sounded on the door. Reaching out with a trembling hand, Nora turned the glass knob.

"Oh, Ingeborge, I—a-a-achooo." The sneeze blew so hard it plugged her ears. She reached to get her handkerchief from her apron pocket but the apron was dangling over the back of a chair. "Cub ind." She tried to smile but instead, at the sight of a smiling, friendly face, Nora collapsed into tears. She shut the door, groped in the pocket of the apron then, in desperation, held the entire apron to her face.

"Oh, my dear, my dear. You look done in. How long have you been sick? How are the children?" All the while she murmured soothing sounds, Ingeborge patted Nora's heaving shoulders.

Kaaren stood, wide-eyed, in the center of the tumbled room.

"Here, now. You sit down in this chair and I'll get you a cup of coffee." Ingeborge pushed Nora down onto the chair. On her way to the cupboard, she removed her hat. With two cups of coffee in hand, she sat down in the chair next to Nora. "Now, tell me all that's happened." As Nora talked, Ingeborge removed her heavy wool coat and beckoned for Kaaren to come sit on her lap.

Nora poured out her miseries—the baby's eating every two hours, the colds and, because of the coughing, her fear of the fever.

"And what about Carl?" Ingeborge smoothed the strands of hair off Nora's flushed, hot face.

"Him? I never see him. Only at mealtime. He never says anything. Only scolds me when Kaaren does not speak English."

"Me say '*Uff da.*' " Kaaren nodded solemnly.

"Oh, you sweetie." Ingeborge hugged the child and kissed her cheek. "I could eat you up."

Kaaren smiled until a cough choked her.

"Well, I know what you need." Ingeborge stroked Nora's arm. "Bed. You wash your face and go crawl into bed. I can stay until late afternoon. I think some rest without worrying is what Doctor Harmon would order."

"Are you sure?" Nora croaked around the lump in her throat.

"I'm sure." Ingeborge slid Kaaren to the floor and then stood up. She took Nora's hand and pulled her upright. "Go, now."

"Peder . . . ?"

"I can see where you have things. We'll do fine. Now go."

Nora did not need to be told a third time. She poured water from the reservoir into a basin, washed her face and hands, and stumbled into the bedroom. She took time to put on her nightgown and then crawl under the covers.

"Thank you, Lord," she mumbled before sleep claimed her.

The next thing Nora heard was a woman's voice singing. She blinked her eyes, wondering where she was. And who was that singing? She lifted her head and looked around the now familiar room. What was she doing in bed at this time of day? She lay back down, her eyelids too heavy to hold open.

Next, she heard a baby crying. "Peder, I'm coming." She sat up and pushed back the covers. This time she felt awake. This time she remembered that Ingeborge had come to visit—and she was sleeping away their precious minutes together.

"Just in time for a cup of fresh coffee." Ingeborge greeted Nora's entrance into the kitchen with a wide smile. "You sit right here," she pointed to the rocker, "and we can talk some before I have to leave."

"Kaaren and Peder?"

"Both sleeping. You're right about that little one. He does not eat much at a time but he wants his bottle every two hours." She handed Nora the steaming cup. "Maybe it's the cow's milk that does not agree with him. Carl says he cries a lot."

"How would he know?" Nora felt ashamed as soon as she had said the words.

"Tell me, dear, how are things between you and Carl?"

At the kind words, Nora swallowed back the tears that threatened to flow. She rubbed a finger around the rim of her cup. "He won't even look at little Peder. He hardly talks to Kaaren but then, when could he? He's never in the house. I do not know where he keeps himself all the time. Has a lot to do down at the barn, I suppose."

She leaned back in her rocking chair and, with a push, started the soothing rhythm. "Ingeborge, what am I to do?"

"Well, one thing I know. The only thing worse than a stubborn Norwegian is a hard-headed German. Right now, I'd say the man is grieving for his young wife and angry at God for taking her." Ingeborge sighed. "I think death is harder for our men than for us. They feel helpless, like they failed. And what can anyone do?"

"Ummm."

"Give him time and love."

Nora stopped the rocking with a thump. "Love? Remember the agreement? I'm going back to Norway as soon as I can."

"Now, now. I'm talking about the kind of love God asks us to give any suffering being. You have an abundance of that kind of love. I've seen it in all you do."

"Oh." Nora again pushed with her toe.

"Can you do that?" The question came softly.

Nora aimed a halfhearted smile at her friend. "It

would be easier if he were around more."

"True. But perhaps that will change." Ingeborge pulled herself to her feet. "Well, supper is in the oven and the bread will have to go in pretty soon. I hung some of the diapers outside so they can freeze over night."

"How can I ever thank you enough?"

Ingeborge took both their cups to the sink. "Just get better. Everything else will work out in God's good time."

The dog barking and a jingle from a harness announced a visitor.

"That must be my John now. He wanted to visit some of the members that live out in the country and that's why I could come today."

"How ashamed I am. I never even asked how you came to be here."

Ingeborge smiled and patted Nora's cheek. "Let's just give God the thanks that He brought me here for you."

After Reverend Moen and Ingeborge left, the special glow that Nora felt around her heart remained. What a good friend she had. The special feeling stayed through the supper time and after feeding Peder. Carl even played with Kaaren before Nora put the little one to bed. When she came out of the bedroom, he was sitting at the table, reading in the lamplight.

He cleared his throat. "Nora." His voice broke. He cleared his throat again. "Would it be possible that I teach you English? Here . . . in the evening? When you get to feeling better?"

eight

The break came a week later. Nora felt like she had been given a priceless gift. Peder slept for four straight hours in the afternoon and again that night. And he smiled at her when she bathed him. This little round face with the button nose that was usually screwed up in either anger or pain, now opened its mouth and let the sides flutter upwards.

Nora lost her heart. She felt it wing from her chest and join with the baby's. She dried him, between each precious little finger and toe, all the while murmuring love words and praising him when the smile came again, broader this time.

Nora wanted to tell someone. Kaaren? No, she was asleep in a much-needed nap. Carl? He should be the person to rejoice in his son's first smile. But he was out working on the farm someplace—who knew where—and, to this day he had never even peeked into the baby's cradle. He never asked about the mite or even said the baby's name.

She would have to settle for writing to her mother as soon as Peder fell back asleep. Her mother would understand the joy Nora felt. It was as if this little life were her very own. Her son. Her Peder.

Nora put a hand to her heart. A pain stabbed at the thought. No, she was only the housekeeper and, in only a few months she would be returning to Norway. Another would see Peder crawl and take his first step. Carl would marry again and his new wife would take over the care of this home and this family.

The words she said to herself made so much sense. After all, they were the truth and the plan Carl had proposed. Why then did they hurt so much?

That night, when Nora and Carl sat down at the table for the English lesson, Nora found it difficult to concentrate.

First, Carl laid their earlier lessons on the table and they reviewed them. Then, she wrote something in Norwegian and, after making sure he understood what she wanted, Carl wrote the English word beside it. Then, he read it to her. She read the words and they repeated them until she said them correctly.

After the lesson, Nora gathered her courage. "Peder smiled at me today," she said slowly as she wrote the words in Norwegian.

Carl took the paper, read the words, and wrote them in English. After he said them in English, he waited for Nora's response. There was no smile, no change in inflection. Nothing.

Uff da, Nora thought. What an impossible man. She repeated the words aloud but now they were just words—the magic she had felt with Peder's first baby smile was missing.

Why? Nora wanted to scream at him. What is the matter with you? But, instead she watched his hand. The hairs on the back of his hand glinted white in the golden glow of the lamp. They were strong hands with long fingers and hard callouses. How would they feel . . . ?

"Nora." The tone snapped impatience.

"Ah, yah?"

"The lesson? If you do not want to continue, just tell me. I have other things I could be doing."

She lifted her gaze to his.

Eyes stern, he repeated his words. "Peder smiled at me today."

"Yah, and his father might try the same." Nora said in Norwegian as she shoved back her chair and rose to her feet. She finished in English. "Good night, Mr. Detschman.

As she swept into the bedroom, she thought she heard a chuckle behind her but she refused to turn and see. No, she shook her head, it must have been the wind.

The next morning, after waking only once during the night to feed the baby, Nora felt more like herself than she had had for weeks. She had diapers washed and hung out before breakfast. There was a johnny cake baking in the oven and Kaaren was giggling at Nora's funny faces.

When Carl walked in the door with a basket of eggs in one hand and a jug of milk in the other, Nora greeted him with a sunny smile. "Good morning, Carl. Would you care for your coffee now?" She spoke in English.

He brushed past her to set the eggs and milk in the sink and grunted.

No "Thank you." No "Congratulations." Not even a smile. Nora knew just how Kaaren felt whenever she stamped her foot. Only now she would prefer having a certain large, booted foot underneath her stamping. His grunt must have meant yes.

When she wrote to her mother that morning, Nora had a hard time thinking of anything good to say about her employer. She corrected her thoughts—"her husband." What a joke!

So, instead, she told them of March in North Dakota, of the Moens, about Peder's smiles, and Kaaren's antics. She did not write about the weeks of walking the floor and wiping runny noses; of no one to talk to; of the ache in her heart for Norway and home; of a little girl who cried at night for the mother that would never return. Of Carl . . . she said nothing.

A few days later, Nora woke to the sound of dripping water. She slipped out of bed, picked up her wrapper, and, while shoving her arms into the sleeves, went to stand at the window. Dawn had just cracked the dark gray of the eastern sky, tinting the clouds with a promise of gold. The icicles, hanging in dagger points from the roof, now dripped onto the snowbanks below.

Nora cupped her hands around her elbows. She could see the cottonwood trees bending before a wind, a warm wind—if her ears really heard dripping water. The Chinook had arrived. Carl had told her about the warm wind that came unannounced from nowhere and melted the snow away. Spring was coming to North Dakota.

That morning, she hurried about her chores. Maybe, for a change she could wrap up Peder and take the children for a walk down to the barn. She was so tired of staying cooped up in the house. "Today, I'll be free," she sang to Peder as she fed him. After all, they were all healthy again. And the fresh air would do them good.

"I'll be going to Soldall today," Carl announced at the breakfast table. "If you have your letter ready, I will mail it for you."

Nora nodded. She held her breath. Maybe he would ask her and the children to go with him. She watched as he ate his mush with rapid bites. The toast disappeared the same way. Nothing was said about their going.

"Carl, I. . . ." Her words stumbled to a halt. She should not have to ask.

"Yah?"

"Ahh, nothing." She handed him her letter. "Thank you."

She and Kaaren waved in the window but he never even turned his head. With a fluid motion, he stepped up into the wagon-turned-sleigh and flicked the reins. The harness jingled into the distance.

"Silly goose," Nora told herself. "What difference does it make if he is here or gone to town? You do not see him anyway." But the heavy feeling hung over her shoulders like the wooden yoke she used to carry two buckets of water to the garden.

While washing the dishes, she stared out the window. The sun still shone, the warm wind tickled the trees—nothing had changed. When she put the last cup away, the thought hit her. *You wanted Carl to show you around his farm.* She nearly dropped the cup.

"Who needs him!" She hung the dish towel over the line behind the stove. "Come along, Kaaren. We're going down to the barn."

"See cows?" Kaaren scrambled to her feet. "Horse?" She ran to pull her coat off the rack. "Pa's barn?"

"Yah, little one. Pa's barn. You must wait for me. We have to get Peder ready, too."

By the time they were all dressed and out the door, Nora could hardly keep from running down the carefully shoveled path. She wanted to fling herself into the snow and teach Kaaren how to make snow angels. Brownie, the cocoa-and-white fluffy dog, picked up on her exuberance and bounded over the snow, his tongue lolling. His sharp barks made Kaaren laugh, then made Nora laugh, then set a big black crow cawing from the top of the windmill.

"Bird." Kaaren pointed toward the sky.

"Yah, this is a bird." Nora agreed. "A—what is it called in English?" Oh well, she shifted Peder into her other arm and guided Kaaren before her. On to the barn.

Nora inhaled deeply when they stepped through the door into the barn's dim interior. She stood for a moment, letting the aromas wash over her. Cow and hay, grain and horses, manure, leather, all the odors so familiar, be they American or Norwegian.

One of the red-and-white shorthorn cows turned her head in her stanchion and lowed at the newcomers. Nora counted four milking cows. Walking farther, she saw the horse stalls. Overhead, a cat meowed and peered down through the open hayloft door.

The animals and barn showed Carl's good care. The manure had been forked out, hay was in the mangers, and the aisles were swept clean. Even with their dense winter coats, the cows showed evidence of having been brushed and curried. Harnesses hung in perfect order on pegs in the wall. Nothing was out of place.

Nora put the bundled baby down onto a pile of hay and, taking Kaaren by the hand, walked up to the first cow. "So-o, boss," she murmured to reassure the cow who turned friendly eyes their way. She reached through the boards of the stanchion and scratched the cow under the chin.

"See, Kaaren, this is how cows like to be petted." She took the little girl's hand and together they rubbed the cow's silky throat. The cow stretched her nose way out, the better to enjoy the caress. Squatting in the straw, cheek-to-cheek with her charge, Kaaren and Nora giggled together as the cow closed her friendly brown eyes in appreciation.

A bay gelding nickered when they came to his stall. He turned his head, pulling against the rope tied to his halter.

Nora looked around and saw the wooden grain bins against one wall. Together, she and Kaaren lifted a slanted lid to see the golden oats half-filling the bin. Nora pulled her mittens off and scooped out a handful of the grain. "For the horse." Grain clenched in her fist, she motioned Kaaren to stand still while she eased her way past the horse's huge body to reach his head.

The horse lipped the grain from her hand and

whiskered her palm, begging for more. Nora
smoothed his forelock and rubbed under the halter
behind his black-fringed ears. "Oh, you beautiful
thing, you. You must be lonely with your friends
gone. I wonder what your name is." All the while
she talked, she rubbed and stroked. When she inhaled, the smell of horse reminded her again of
home. Some things stayed the same, everywhere.

Sure now that the animal was gentle, she went
back out and, taking Kaaren in her arms, brought
her up to pat the horse, too. Her big hand guided the
little one.

"Pa's horse." Kaaren giggled when the animal
blew in her face. She wrapped her arm around the
back of Nora's neck and leaned against her, cheek-
to-cheek.

Peder began to whimper on his hay nest so Nora
gave the horse one last pat and left the stall. Down
the aisle she found another stall, this one with two
white hogs. She lifted Kaaren up to see over the
wall.

"Pa's pigs." Kaaren announced.

By the time Nora picked Peder up again, he had
switched from whimper to demand. "Hush, now.
We'll go feed you but you must be patient." They
left the barn and dropped the bar into place behind
them.

The windmill squeaked and turned in the wind
above the low building that must be the well house.
Off to the side of the barn other buildings waited to
be explored but Nora walked quickly between the
snowbanks. Peder had been so good he deserved to

eat right away.

Under the onslaught of the Chinook, the snow
quickly melted. Nora watched the calendar as Easter approached. One day, after serving fried pork
chops for dinner, she made a decision.

"Carl."

He stopped drinking his coffee and looked at her
over the rim of his coffee cup.

"Is Easter soon?"

He nodded.

"We go to church?" Nora hated to stumble over
her words but she knew he wanted her to speak
English whenever she could.

He pushed his chair back and set the cup carefully
down on the table. Jaw tight, he grabbed his coat
and strode out the door.

"That must mean 'No.'" She stared after him. At
least he could have answered. She had said the
words right—hadn't she?

In spite of the thundercloud that seemed to have
taken up permanent residence on Carl's forehead,
Nora went ahead with her spring housecleaning.
Her home must be shiny clean for the risen Christ.
Laundry danced on the clothesline, rugs took their
beating without a murmur, windows sparkled and
welcomed their clean curtains.

On Saturday, while Carl was in town, she poured
water into the washtub in front of the stove and,
after giving Kaaren a bath, took one herself. She left
the tub of water for Carl to use and disappeared into
the bedroom with the children.

The next morning, the tub was gone. Nora wished Carl had rinsed away that stern look when he had washed his hair.

"Christ is risen, He is risen indeed." Nora whispered the words to the sun on Easter morning. "Thank you, Father for loving us and sending Your Son to die. And rise again. He is risen."

When she thought of missing church, the organ, and the hymns, the joy of Easter dimmed. So, Nora refused to let the thoughts of what she was missing bother her.

Instead, in her mind, she repeated the words over and over. *Jesus Christ is risen today.* Even Carl's scowl when Kaaren spilled her milk failed to drown out Nora's inner chorus.

That evening after supper, Nora and Kaaren sat at the table reading a schoolbook Carl had brought back from town. Nora read the English slowly but Kaaren did not mind. She pointed a chubby finger at the pictures, naming each object. When she got bored, she slid to the floor and ambled off to the bedroom.

A few minutes later, she came back, dragging her doll. She pulled on Nora's skirt. "Ma."

Nora felt her stomach fall clear to her knees. She focused hard on her book, hoping and praying that Carl had not heard. She scooped Kaaren up onto her lap. But the deed was done. She did not have to turn to see his face—his thudding footsteps on the stairs told her what he was thinking.

Kaaren put her tiny palm on top of the book, now closed, on the table. "Ma's book."

"Auntie Nora's book." She covered the small hand with her own.

Kaaren shook her head. She peered up at Nora with eyes the blue of a summer lake. "Ma's book."

With a shaking hand, Nora pressed the dear little head to her chest. What would she do about this latest folly? Did Carl think she taught Kaaren to say that? Didn't he know that she would never do such a thing? She leaned her cheek on the top of Kaaren's head. But then, what did Carl really know of her at all?

Nora crawled into bed that night with a heavy heart. How could a day that began with heavenly singing, end on such a sour note?

nine

Two days had passed and he had not spoken to her. Nora felt her temper simmering like a kettle about to boil over. She stifled the urge to slam the lid of the stove back in place—or the oven door. In fact, she knew if she stepped outside after the sun went down, her cheeks would freeze in the smile she forced past her clenched teeth.

She heard her mother's soft voice. "*Ah, Nora, do not let the sun go down on your anger.*" But Nora knew that that had referred to keeping a happy marriage. And this . . . this contract she was caught in certainly could not be called a marriage in any terms she knew of.

But this is what you agreed to, the cool voice of reason reminded her. *So you could go back to Norway, remember?*

"Talking to myself, hearing voices. You think my mind is going?" The gray-striped cat in her lap looked up and yawned, showing white dagger teeth and a raspy pink tongue. She stretched her front paws way out, claws digging into Nora's knee, then curled back up and resumed the rumbling purr that could probably be heard across the room.

Nora set the chair to rocking, letting her thoughts fly back over the last few weeks. Whenever she thought of Carl, his anger came to mind. Had she done anything to make him mad? Well, she tried not to, that was for certain, but he either snapped at her or ignored her. No, that's not all true, she corrected herself. The English lessons have mostly been peaceful times.

Was it his sorrow that made him so . . . so . . . she searched for the best word. Angry, yes. But lost? She stroked the cat's back. Lost, yes, but more like an animal that has been wounded and strikes out at anyone who tries to help. She nodded.

So, what do I do? She let her mind float again, like a thistle seed caught on a summer's breeze. The answer came strong and clear. *Pray for him. Pray for him daily. Pray for him when he spitefully uses you.* A verse from her confirmation time, part of the "blesseds" that she so loved.

Silence reigned in the kitchen, a peace that gilded each chair and shelf, that glistened on the stove, and sparkled in the window. Even the cat's purring ceased. Nora felt that peace slip into her heart and fill it to bursting. "Bless this poor hurting man, oh my heavenly Father. Bring healing to his broken heart and bring him back to You." She whispered the words, as if loud sounds might disturb the moment.

A meadowlark sang from the fence, its song fluting on the morning air.

Nora lifted the hem of her apron and wiped the corner of her eye. "Thank You." The words had to squeeze past the lump in her throat. "I promise to pray for Carl everyday. Amen."

After supper that evening, Nora brought out her books and paper and put them on the table. When

Carl came back into the house after having checked on the animals, Nora met him with a cup of coffee.

"Please." She nodded to the chair she had already pulled out and extended the cup with both hands. "English lessons I want."

"Nora, I'm really tired, I. . . ."

Nora held the cup and threw all her heart into the smile. "Please."

"Oh, all right." Carl took the cup and sat down at the table. He took a sip and set the cup down on the table. "Let's see where we were."

Nora sent another "Thank you" heavenward and slipped into her own chair. She took up the pencil and wrote, "When do the roses bloom?"

Carl looked at her with a question in his eyes. "Roses?"

Nora nodded. "I love roses." She repeated the word he had used carefully.

Carl shook his head. "No roses here. Wild roses in June."

Nora shrugged her confusion. What did he mean?

"Let's review what we've done before." He pulled out pages they had written on in the past and pointed to the sentences. Nora had been practicing. She said them all, correctly.

"Good." He nodded. One lock of golden hair fell over his forehead.

Nora had the urge to reach out and brush it back. Instead she pulled herself to her feet and went for the coffeepot to refill their cups.

Nora sat down and wrote another sentence. "I want to plant a garden."

Carl wrote the English and together they repeated the words.

He nodded. "Soon. I'll plow up the garden, soon."

That night, as she knelt by her bed, Nora remembered her promise. She smiled to herself as she slipped between the covers—praying for the man wasn't so difficult when she didn't feel like pouring coffee on his head.

One morning, Nora had another surprise. Brownie's barking announced company and, when Nora threw open the door, the entire Moen family waved from their light buggy. Reverend Moen reined his horse to a halt and, after climbing down, helped Ingeborge and the children to get out.

Nora flew down the steps and met them on the walk. "Come in, come in. Oh, you do not know how happy I am to see you." Her words tumbled over each other like puppies playing in the sun. She hugged Ingeborge and reached out to shake hands with Reverend Moen. "Come in."

"You look wonderful," Ingeborge said as she tucked her arm into Nora's. "And how is that man of yours now?"

"Carl's out riding the fenceline to make sure none of the cows can get out." She turned to Reverend Moen. "I'm sure he will be so happy to see you."

"Good. I'll return to gather my family later this afternoon. Maybe he'll be back then." Reverend Moen set a basket on the porch and turned to leave. "You all have a good visit now."

They waved him away and walked into the house.

"I brought you some things." Ingeborge handed baby James to Nora and went back outside for the basket. "If the coffee is hot, we can share the cookies right now." She plunked the basket on the table and began removing her gifts. "Jam, bread, *spekemat*, and cheese. One of the church members brought me this the other day. I thought you might appreciate it, too."

"Oh, like home." Nora sniffed the wrapped piece of strong-smelling cheese. "Thank you."

"And sour cream cookies. Mary cut them out for me."

"I put the sugar on," said Knute. "Come on, Mary. Let's play ball on the porch."

Kaaren took her finger out of her mouth long enough to shove her hands into her coat sleeves and followed the others out the door.

"Stay out of the mud," Nora reminded them. "Kaaren, you hear me?"

While a "Yes, Ma," trailed back, Nora looked at Ingeborge and shrugged.

"And here's the best gift of all." Ingeborge drew an envelope from the bottom of the basket.

Nora reached for the letter. "From home. Oh, thank you." She slipped it into her apron pocket to be read and savored later.

With baby James unwrapped from his quilts and lying on another one on the floor and Peder still sleeping, Nora and Ingeborge sat down with their coffee to catch up on the news.

They talked until it was time to fix dinner and continued to talk while preparing the meal. They

were both feeding their babies when Nora heard
Carl out on the porch, talking with the children.

"All right if these funny people I found on the
porch go down to play in the hayloft after dinner?"
he asked as he came in the door.

"That would be wonderful," Ingeborge replied.

Nora could not say a word—shock locked her
tongue.

Dinner was a lively affair. And quick. Carl even
gave up his second cup of coffee to take the children
down to play in the barn.

"I have a favor to ask," Nora said when they sat
down again.

"What?"

"Will you write the English words to "Jesus Loves
Me." I want to teach Kaaren to sing it but Carl
insists we speak English. So many things I can't
give her because I speak Norwegian."

"Of course I will. But you are learning some?"

"Yah, Carl and Kaaren, they teach me." She went
on to describe her evening lessons.

"And Kaaren calls you 'Ma?' "

Nora nodded. "Carl was not pleased but I've tried
to tell her where her ma is. And he will not talk with
her about it. He hardly talks to her at all."

"What a shame." Ingeborge laid her hand on
Nora's arm. "He used to have a wonderful smile—
Anna would tease him into smiling and laughing.
They were happy, those two."

"And now he says nothing. He works himself into
a stupor. You should see the barn. I think he has
scrubbed the walls and even the floor. I'm sure the

machinery is the same. Every buckle on the horses'
harnesses shines."

"Men are like that. Sometimes I think God gave
us heavy work so we can live through life's sorrows.
And men more so than women—they can't cry."

Nora nodded. She picked up her cup and sipped
the cooling drink. "But crying and laughing again
makes the sorrow easier to bear."

"Yah. That and praying."

The silence, sweet and comfortable, lengthened.
The clock on the wall ticked away the moments. A
robin sang from the cottonwood tree beyond the
fence. Coal whooshed as it sank in the firebox.

Ingeborge roused herself first. "Now, to 'Jesus
Loves Me.' Do you have paper handy?"

By the time Reverend Moen came to retrieve his
brood, Nora had most of the English words to the
song locked away in her heart. And, to refresh her
memory, the carefully written words. After they
left, she studied the letters. Maybe this new language was not so ugly after all.

That night, as she brushed the hayseeds from
Kaaren's hair, she hummed the song. Kaaren chattered away about the hayloft with Nora listening
carefully to pick out words she knew. "Pa's barn"
and "hayloft" she understood and giggles were a
universal language.

Later, after the English language session was finished, Carl brought a box from the pantry and set it
on the table. "Go ahead," he said with a motion.
"Open it. These are seeds for the garden. I will plow
tomorrow."

"Plow?" Nora tasted the strange word.

Carl wrote it down so Nora could look the word up in the dictionary. More and more she was able to find the words she needed by referring to the dictionary. She read the meaning, "To turn the soil with a tool."

"Then we plant?" She gestured to the seeds.

"After the ground dries. Then the harrow. Plant next week."

"Thank you." She turned her attention to the packets of seeds. While she could not read the labels, she did not need to. Peas, beans, corn, pumpkins—all were easily recognized. She held up one packet of very small seeds.

"Carrots." Carl identified it as well as the others. "Turnips, rutabaga, lettuce. Potatoes are down in the cellar. I'll buy onions when I go to town."

Nora nodded. Her fingers picked through the packets as if they had a delicate life of their own. Her own garden. She would plant and weed and water and they would have fresh vegetables. And some to preserve.

After her prayers for Carl that night, she slipped into bed with a smile still on her face. Her last thought wiped it away—by the time the garden was ready to eat, she would be on her way back to Norway.

She could not bear to remain in the house the morning Carl brought up the team hitched to a plow and started turning the soil. Rich black curls of dirt folded over in perfectly straight lines, running north and south. She reached down and picked up a handful of loam, clenching her fist and then letting the dirt crumble back to the earth. She breathed in the aroma of the rich soil, the promise of spring and of rebirth.

"Easy, now," Carl sang out to the team as they turned another corner. The harness jingled and the horses snorted as they leaned into their collars.

Nora watched when they started back toward her. Sun glinted off Carl's bright golden hair, the one lock falling over his broad forehead.

Like her, he raised his face to the sun, then brushed the strand back with his forearm. His shirt sleeves were rolled back, exposing skin already turning pink from the sun.

"Ma?" Kaaren tugged on Nora's skirt.

"Yah?" Nora left off gazing at the man on the plow and bent to see what Kaaren wanted.

"See?" Between two careful fingers, Kaaren held up an angleworm she had rescued from the turned earth. Nora held out her hand and Kaaren placed it on the flattened palm.

What is the English word here, thought Nora as she joined Kaaren in oohing over the creature.

"Show Pa?" Kaaren looked up, her eyes dancing with delight.

"Yah." Nora nodded. "And maybe he'll tell me what to call it," she smiled. Who could keep from smiling on a day like this one?

"I'm going into town," Carl announced the next morning after breakfast. "You need anything?"

Nora thought quickly. Kaaren needed new dresses and they were nearly out of sugar. How she would love to go along and visit with Ingeborge. Maybe he would ask her.

But Carl only wrote down the things she listed for him, including cloth for new dresses. When he drove out the yard, he was by himself. She and Kaaren were left on the porch, waving goodbye.

"Come, little one. We'll bake some cookies and go down to the barn to see the new calf."

Kaaren stared wistfully at the barn. "Go in the hayloft?" She raised hopeful eyes to Nora. "Jump in the hay?"

"We'll see." Nora turned back to the kitchen. "Cookies, first."

Later, Nora wrapped bread and jelly sandwiches in one napkin, fresh cinnamon cookies in another, and poured milk into a pint jar. Then she wrapped Peder in a blanket and the three of them started for the barn.

The new red-and-white calf bawled from his pen as soon as they swung open the door to the otherwise empty barn. The cows were out to pasture, Carl was driving the horses, and the pigs could be heard rooting around in their lean-to at the side of the barn.

"Up." Nora pointed to the ladder, slanted from the floor to the door in the ceiling to the hayloft. She gave Kaaren a boost and stood beside the ladder until the little girl scrambled out of sight. Nora climbed up halfway and laid their lunch on the smooth boards of the hayloft floor. When she, with Peder in one arm, reached the upper floor, she stopped a moment just to look.

Rafters met in the peaked roof, high and dim in the dust-laden light. Much of the grass hay had already been fed to the livestock but the densely packed fodder still covered about half the floor to a height of several feet. A pitchfork stabbed into the hay stood erect just like an empty flagpole.

Kaaren ran across the floor to the hay and slipped and slid until she perched on top of the mound. Then, she sat on the edge, legs straight in front and, like sledding down a hill, slipped down the incline. She landed with a thump, giggling and calling "See, Ma. Come, slide." She turned and scrambled back up. This time, she lay back flat and slid down again.

"Well, this hardly makes up for the hills in Norway but we'll make our fun where we can," Nora muttered to herself as she laughed and encouraged Kaaren. When Nora left Peder on the hay and slid down the hay pile, Kaaren laughed and raced back up.

Nora lay back on the hay and looked up at the dust motes dancing in the light streaming through the high window. On the other end of the barn, was a square door. It took up most of the wall and was meant to be opened to bring in the new hay. What a wonderful place to have a dance. When she thought about it, she missed the dances at home. People laughing, whirling, and tapping to the music. One thing Norwegians knew how to do—dance and have a good time.

Kaaren plunked down beside her. When Nora did not get up, the little girl snuggled down and laid her head on Nora's shoulder. "Hungry, Ma. Eat, now?" She patted Nora's cheek with her grubby hand.

"Yah, we'll eat." With Peder propped in her arms and Kaaren sitting cross-legged in perfect imitation of her, they devoured their dinner. Between bites, Nora sang the first line of the new song she had learned. "Jesus loves me this I know" rose to the rafters and echoed back to form a heavenly chorus.

When Carl returned home that evening, he brought in the supplies. One little sack he handed to Kaaren.

She carefully opened the top of it and squealed. "Candy. Yummm." She plopped down on the rug and stuck one piece in her mouth. Sucking on it took all her concentration.

Nora opened her package carefully, too. "So much?" She held up the light blue cotton material with small, dark blue flowers.

"You need a summer dress, too."

"Thank you." Nora held the fabric up to her cheek. "Is beautiful."

"You're welcome." He continued to move packages around until he pulled something out from behind the flour sack. He set the burlap packet on the table in front of Nora. "For you." He spoke like he had a rough patch in his throat.

She stared at him, wondering what else there could be. Carefully, she folded back the edges of the burlap. Inside, the roots still planted in a clump of moist soil, was the start of a rosebush. Tiny red nubbins, ready to sprout into new growth, glowed on three, dark green, thorny stems.

Tears filled her eyes and blurred the gift. "Thank you." With the back of her hand, she dashed away the falling drops. When she raised her gaze to Carl's, he dropped his.

The silence vibrated between them like a fine piano wire tapped by the hammer. Unheard, unseen—the music crept into their hearts.

Carl cleared his throat and the silence tinkled to the floor to lie in quivering fragments. "Uhhmm." He started to say something but had to clear his throat again. "I'll be putting the horses away . . . and milking. . . .If you could have supper ready later?"

"Yah, I will." Nora whispered, never taking her eyes off his face. While there was no smile, she realized the lines between his eyebrows had smoothed away.

The next day, while Nora dug a hole by the front porch and planted her rosebush, Carl readied the garden spot. Now the soil was loose and flat, clods breaking down as the team and harrow cut pass after pass across the land.

"You can plant now." Carl reined the horses in and stepped off the harrow to stand in front of Nora. "The hoe is in the cellar." He made hoeing motions with his hands and pointed to the cellar door slanted against the side of the house. "After dinner, I'll begin plowing the fields." He pointed off to the east. Stubble from the previous fall lay gray on the land. "Wheat first, then oats, and finally, corn. Maybe potatoes, too." He took off his broad-brimmed, black hat and the teasing breeze lifted his hair.

Nora stood transfixed. He glowed—burnished by

the sun and the wind—his love for the land, part and parcel of his soul, shining from his eyes.

She looked out across the fallow land, flat as her eyes could see. A meadowlark soared and sang above them, it's notes trilling down like bits of sunlight to be caught in her heart.

Later, serving the dinner, Nora laid one hand on his shoulder while she set a plate on the table in front of him. The need to touch him, to feel the strength of this man, welled up from that same place within her that hoarded the sunbeams. How right it felt.

"Thank you, Nora, for the good food." Carl pushed back his chair. "See you tonight."

Nora stared after him. Was God working His miracle?

Nora stacked the dishes in the sink and fed Peder. Then, taking a shawl, she settled him in it crosswise and, knotting two opposite corners together, formed a sling that she lifted over her head. She tied another shawl the opposite way and now the baby was clasped snugly against her chest.

With her hands free, she picked up the box of seeds. On the porch waited the hoe that Carl had brought up from the cellar. "Come Kaaren, we are going planting."

The sun had passed the midafternoon mark when Nora looked up from her labors at the sound of the dog barking. She shaded her eyes, looking off to the west where the sound came from. Two men strode across the field.

"We have company," she announced to Kaaren

who was busily digging a trench with a stick she had found. Nora watched them come closer. Dark hair, long, held back with a band. Dark faces, tattered shirts, leather leggings. One carried a rifle.

"Indians." Nora clutched the baby to her. All she had ever read and heard of the thieving, murdering, American savages flooded her mind.

ten

"God, help!" Nora leaned over and grasped Kaaren by the hand, jerking her to her feet.

The Indians stopped at the edge of the garden. They stared at her.

She stared at them. Her heart pounded in her chest, loud enough she was sure that they could hear. "You must welcome strangers," her mother's words could barely be heard over the bellows of her lungs.

Nora tried to swallow. Not even enough juice to spit, let alone swallow—or talk. What good would talk do anyway? What language did they speak? Certainly not Norwegian. She stepped forward like she had a board stuck to her spine. "Hello."

Black eyes did not blink. The taller one surveyed her from the crown of her braids, to her boot tips that peeked out from under her black skirt, and back up again, slowly. When he muttered something, the shorter one shrugged.

Welcome strangers, welcome strangers. What did you do when strangers came, especially if they are the type that might take your hair and scalp with them when they left? She clamped her teeth against the bile that rose from her stomach, threatening to make her disgrace herself. What do you do with company like this?

Offer them food, of course. "You, eat? Drink?" If

that slight motion of the tall one's head was agreement, Nora needed no second response.

"Come." She clutched Kaaren's hand and strode across the planted rows, girl in tow, head high. "Never show fear," was her father's advice for dealing with both strangers and animals. Nora fought to hang onto those words of wisdom.

"Sit." She motioned to the porch steps and, without looking back to see if they obeyed, strode with Kaaren across the porch and through the door, letting the screen door slam behind her. She untied the sling contraption from around her shoulders and laid Peder in his cradle. Back in the kitchen, her hands shook so much she could scarcely pick up the knife. She sneaked glances at the door, sure that it would slam open at any moment and they would come to. . . .She sliced bread and poured milk into cups. With bread, milk, leftover chicken that she had planned to have for supper, and cookies on the plates, she paused at the door.

The dark-skinned men sat on the stairs like she had ordered, leaning against the posts with their arms draped across their bent knees. One carved on a piece of wood with a knife that glinted in the sun. The gun rested against the outside of the porch, right near the owner's leg.

Please, God. . . . Nora never finished the prayer as she pushed the door open and crossed the porch. "Here." She handed each of them a plate, then dug into her apron pocket for forks. When she held the silver out, they ignored her and ate with their hands.

Nora eased her way backward and, fumbling with

her hands behind her, opened the screen door and slipped inside. She stood watching them through the screen.

The taller man scraped his plate clean with the bread and raised his cup in her direction.

"M-more?" If she could just quit stuttering.

He nodded.

She brought the jug out and refilled both their cups.

When they drained the cups, they set them and the plates on the floor. Slowly, they stood. The tall man picked up his gun. The shorter one slid his knife back into its sheath.

Nora now knew what the rabbit felt like when facing a fox.

"Thank you, Carl's new woman." The tall man spoke in better English than she did. He nodded— once. Their long strides eating up the ground, the two Indians headed east.

Nora felt a gurgle of laughter churning in her middle and pleading to be let out. She stepped out onto the porch and bent to pick up the plates. As she stood again, she looked out across the land. The taller Indian raised a hand high in the air—and waved.

When she told Carl the story that night after dinner, she watched his face carefully. His lip twitched, his eyes crinkled. He had a dimple in his right cheek. When she repeated the Indian's "Thank you, Carl's new woman," Carl bent over double. The laughter exploded from him like a shot from a cannon; the kitchen echoed with his chortles.

Kaaren giggled along and banged her spoon on

the table.

Nora sat back and let the music of his mirth flow over, around, and through her. She was not sure which she was laughing at more—her story or his enjoyment of her story.

When he wiped his eyes with the heel of his hands, she said with a lift of her chin, "He say better English than me."

Carl dug into his back pocket for a handkerchief then he blew his nose and shook his head, laughter still quivering in his shoulders. "The tall one is called One Horse and his shorter brother is Night of the Fox. They've been walking through here ever since I bought the farm. Sometimes, I find a deer carcass as a gift. Sometimes, they sleep in my barn. You could say we've become friends the last few years." The grin split his face again. "All the Indian stories you've heard, that was long ago."

"Next time I'll know."

The corners of his mouth remained tipped up all through the English lesson and while Nora tucked both Peder and Kaaren into bed. When Nora returned to the kitchen, she took her place in the rocker and picked up the pieces of blue-flowered material she had cut out for Kaaren's dress. In between stitches, she sneaked peeks at the man caught in the circle of lamplight. His smile had faded but so had the lines from his nose to his mouth and those in his forehead.

"Thank you, Father," she prayed that night on her knees. "He is so beautiful when he laughs." She rested her chin on her clasped hands. "But, next time, maybe he could laugh with me instead of at me." Her lips curved up at the thought. "But thanks, no matter what. I'm not choosy."

Before she drifted off, the rest of a Bible verse her mother used to recite floated through her mind. *"Welcome strangers for you may be entertaining angels unawares." Funny looking angels*, she thought. *And I was so scared. She pictured the scene in the garden again. But, it was worth it.*

Within a week, Nora had her garden planted. New growth on her rosebush jutted out several inches with more new leaves unfolding everyday. When she looked toward the horizon, newborn grass sprouted, cloaking the unplowed land in green velvet.

"When you look across the prairie," she wrote her sister Clara, "you can see clear into next month. While I miss the mountains and fjords, I can see the beauty in this part of God's creation, also. It is not a forgotten land as I had first thought."

When Carl drove into town one day, he took her letter and returned with another. This one was in answer to his advertisement for a housekeeper.

"Bah. She can't speak English, either," he growled after dropping the letter onto the table. He flicked the paper with his fingers. "Why did she even bother to write? I said specifically that the woman must speak English."

When Nora brought out her papers for their lesson, he waved her away. "I'm too tired to concentrate on that tonight." He heaved himself out of his chair. "Good night."

Nora could hear his weariness in the measured

tread with which he climbed the stairs.

Sitting under the lamplight, stitching away on Kaaren's dress, Nora searched her heart. Was it joy she felt when he said the woman would not work out? Surely not. Her dream was to return to Norway and she would not be able to do that until Carl found someone to take her place.

Each day Peder seemed to do something new. He not only smiled now but laughed when Nora blew on his round tummy. He waved pudgy arms and, when he reached for an object, sometimes he got it. When Nora laid him on a quilt either on the floor or outside on the grass, Kaaren would dangle a rubber jar ring or the bright red stuffed dog Nora had sewn for him. Hearing them laughing together always made Nora smile.

Carl ignored them.

"How can he?" Nora fumed one night after seeing him take a wide track around the two little ones on the floor. Kaaren was on her tummy, legs waving in the air while she and Peder laughed and chattered, her mimicking Peder's "goo's" and "ga ga's."

One evening, Nora sat rocking and feeding Peder his bottle when she heard a thump, bump . . . silence . . . and then a scream to strike fear in any mother's heart.

Carl leaped to his feet, picked the screaming Kaaren up off the floor at the foot of the stairs and tried to comfort her.

"No!" She arched her back and screamed louder. "Ma-a-a! I want my ma!"

Nora could see blood streaming from a wound above Kaaren's right eye. She stood, handed Peder along with his bottle to Carl, and took the little girl over to the sink. With a cold cloth pressed to the site to stop the bleeding, Nora murmured words of comfort. She turned to see Carl, wooden-faced, holding the baby stiffly in his arms.

Peder began to whimper, wanting the remainder of his supper. Without looking at his son, Carl walked into the bedroom, laid the bundle on the bed as if it were no more than a package from the store, and stalked out the door.

Nora struggled between vexation and pity. She wrapped a bandage over the tiny cut above Kaaren's eye. Then she retrieved Peder and resumed feeding him, still petting and comforting Kaaren.

Vexation swelled into fury. _That man! That insufferable, hardheaded, coldhearted_—she ran out of words harsh enough to describe him. _Who did he think he was anyway? Other people in this world lose their loved ones and they still love those left. How could he not love such a darling baby as Peder?_

"I will not pray for him tonight." She knelt by the bed, hoping to hear Carl's footsteps returning but was almost glad when they did not. "God, You don't _really_ want me to pray for him, do You?" She listened to the silence. Outside somewhere, an owl hooted in its nightly hunting forays. The breeze fluffed the lace curtains at the open window.

She started to climb into bed. "Oh, fiddle." She knelt back down and scrunched her eyes closed, her teeth snapping together between words. "Please bless Carl and help him get through this time of sorrow. Make him love his sweet little son and. . . ."

She stopped to think. Nothing more came. "Amen."

She climbed back into bed and pulled up the covers. "So there." The silence crept back into the room. Was that God, chuckling on the breeze? Nora turned over to sleep, a smile curving her lips.

With May, the beans leaped from the ground. Carrot feathers waved in their rows and the potatoes pushed up corrugated leaves to find the sun.

Nora leaned on her hoe, pride in her handiwork evident in the smile on her face. She pushed back the straw hat she had found in the cellar and wiped the sweat from her forehead. What her garden needed now was a slow-falling, soaking rain. She eyed the gray clouds mounding in the west. A lightning fork stabbed the sky.

"At least a storm can't catch you by surprise here," she said with a shrug. "And here I am talking to myself again. Better start giving myself orders, too. So get over there and take the wash off the line. It's been wet once today. It doesn't need to be wet again." She suited actions to her words and paused only long enough to watch rain fall in gray veils across the land. She dashed to the house with a full basket just as the first drops pelted the dust.

Carl galloped the team up to the barn, the harrow left in the fields. Nora stood on the porch. "What happened to him?" Brownie whined at her feet.

"Are you all right?" she yelled above the rising wind.

At his wave, she turned back into the house. Expecting him to come up for coffee, she stoked the embers and added coal to the fire. Maybe she should start an early supper. Even though the clock said four, the sky said dusk.

She crossed to the open door and, through the screen door watched huge, fat raindrops pound the earth. She shook her head. "Doesn't this country ever do anything gently?"

"Ma?" Kaaren meandered out of the bedroom, rubbing sleep from her eyes. She leaned against Nora's skirt until Nora picked her up and set the little girl on her hip.

Lightning forked beyond the barn and in a few moments thunder crashed. Nora stood in awe at the heavenly display. She heard the rain gurgle in the downspouts and into the cistern under the house. Lightning lit the sky again.

"Pretty." Kaaren leaned her head against Nora's shoulder. When the thunder boomed, she flinched, then giggled. Nora could already hear that the storm was moving to the east of them. Now, the rain fell in billowing skirts, gentle and kind. The cool breeze felt good.

She left the doorway and finished grinding the dark beans for coffee. By the time Carl stepped onto the porch, the aroma of coffee brewing floated out to meet him.

"Smells wonderful." He sniffed appreciatively and hung his hat on the rack.

"Pretty lights." Kaaren pointed out the window. "Big boom."

Carl tousled her hair with one hand before picking her up. "Did you like it?"

She nodded, her blue eyes grave. "Hungry, Pa?"

At his nod, she smiled, "Me, too."

"Sit down. I have cookies. Supper will be soon."

This time, when Nora rested her hand on Carl's shoulder, she felt a tremor go up her arm—he had leaned into her gentle pressure. She finished pouring the coffee and took her own chair. When Carl smiled at her it was as if the skies had parted and the sun beamed down to melt the frost that had stilled the heart.

"Thank you," was all he said but, with the smile, it was enough.

Nora rejoiced in the moments Carl spent with Kaaren. Though few and far between since he was in the fields at dawn and did not return to milk the cows until dark, the little one now met him at the door with a welcome grin. Even though he was so tired he would fall asleep at the table, he took time to listen to Kaaren's chatter and admire her new dress.

Of Peder, he never questioned or mentioned.

One afternoon, Nora moved the rocker and cradle out to the porch so she could sew and enjoy the sun at the same time. For a time, Kaaren played quietly at her feet but soon demanded a song and a story. Nora stuck her needle into the material of the bodice for her new dress and set it in the basket at her feet.

"Here we go." After hoisting Kaaren up onto her lap, Nora picked up the Bible written in English that she had in the same basket and turned to the Gospel of Matthew. Slowly, she read the story of Jesus and the children. Softly, she began singing, "Jesus loves me this I know." Kaaren joined in and together they finished the chorus.

"More." Kaaren leaned back against Nora's

shoulder and Nora closed her eyes. They sang it again. "Yes, Jesus loves me, yes Jesus. . . ."

"What are you doing?" Carl's voice cut like a knife.

Nora felt like she had been stabbed. Her eyes flew open to clash with his, limpid pond against glacier. Confusion to fury.

Karen stuck her finger in her mouth and whimpered, her chin quivering as she stared from her father to Nora.

"Pa-a-a!" Her wail floated on the breeze spun up by his leaving.

"Shhh." Nora comforted her. "You sit here in my chair and take care of Peder. I will come back."

At Kaaren's nod, Nora rose to her feet and set the little girl back in the chair. Then, she gathered her skirts and ran down the path to the barn.

Carl had the horses backed up on either side of the wagon shaft and was hooking the traces when she stopped in front of him.

"Why are you angry?" She stumbled over the words, wishing she could use Norwegian instead of English.

He ignored her, continuing the harnessing.

"Carl!" She might as well have been talking to the barn door.

When he lifted a foot to mount the wagon, she placed a hand on his arm. "Carl, what did I do?"

He spun around, reins in his hand. "Do? The Bible. That song. How can you sing and worship a God Who kills innocent mothers and children?"

eleven

"But your son lived!"

Carl stepped forward, towering over her in his fury. "But his mother didn't! She died and he might as well have."

"What are you saying?" She clenched her hands in the sides of her skirt. She would rather be pummeling his chest.

"I'm saying I don't want you teaching my daughter those songs and filling her head with lies about a God Who loves her."

"But Jesus—God loves us all. He will help you, if you ask."

"I don't need His kind of help."

"But, Carl." She placed her hand on his arm.

He threw her hand off, the wind of it whistling by her cheek. Leaping up onto the wagon, he flicked the reins. "Ha, boys." Without a look back, he drove down the lane.

Nora stared after him, tears burning behind her eyes. "Oh, God help you poor, poor man." She bit the knuckles on her right hand, her left pressed against her throat. "Only God can help you. Father, please take away Carl's bitterness. Bring him Your love. Restore his faith. Father, forgive me. I cannot do what he asks."

Dust from the wagon's churning wheels hung in the still air. It smelled like despair.

Nora opened the barn door and wandered inside. Clean floors, harnesses draped over pegs in perfect order—all showed a man who cared about his farm. Outside, the fat cows switched their tails in the shade of the barn, a newly replaced fence post anchored a gate that swung smoothly on oiled hinges. She wandered over to the pigpen. The sow and her piglets lay on a pile of straw under a roof to keep off the hot sun. Carl loved his animals.

On the way up to the house, she thought about him . . . tossing Kaaren in the air to make her laugh . . . of his sitting with the chattering child, answering her myriad questions. Yes, he loved his family . . . the fields, green and growing . . . the rosebush he had brought her. Here was a man with love locked away in his heart, with wounds deep in his soul. Where was the key to that lock? What salve would heal his hurt?

Back in the chair with Kaaren on her lap, she rocked and thought—and prayed.

May flowed into June and Carl continued working from before dawn until long after dark. With the fields planted and up, the cultivating began. Endless hours of riding the metal seat of the cultivator pulled behind two sweating horses, their heads bobbing in time to the plodding of their hooves.

Nora walked everywhere with Peder in the sling and Kaaren clutching her hand or running ahead. One day, they found wild strawberries along a fence row. She made preserves from the berries and baked biscuits for shortcake.

Carl only grunted when served the treats.

Nora was not sure if the grunt meant "Thank you" or "Give me more." She didn't.

The temper she had prayed so earnestly over for so many years, simmered and, once in a while, spit.

Haying season began. One evening, Carl drove the team up after dark and found Nora milking the cows. Kaaren was playing in the aisle; Peder was sleeping peacefully on a mound of hay.

"I didn't ask you to do this," he said.

Nora continued to squeeze and pull, the milk singing into the bucket. "I know." She kept her forehead against the cow's red flank.

"Take the children up to the house. I will finish."

"Carl Detschman, you are the most stubborn, bullheaded, prideful man I have ever had the misfortune to know." Nora reverted to Norwegian. She did not know enough of the right words in English. She pulled a bit too forcefully and got a mouthful of cow's tail.

"Nora."

"No, *you* take Kaaren and your son Peder to the house. Maybe you'll have time to soak your head before I get there." She stripped the last of the milk from each teat and, setting the bucket aside, rose to her feet. "*I* have one more cow to milk."

Carl stepped back before she could trod on his feet.

Nora picked up a clean bucket and her stool and plunked them down beside the next cow. "So-o-o, boss." She settled the bucket between her skirted knees and her head into the cow's flank. With the same easy rhythm, she squeezed and pulled, ringing the milk into the bucket.

She refused to look up when she heard Carl leave. She did not tell him her hands and arms were cramping either. When she peeked over her shoulder, the quilt where Peder had lain was gone.

Nora hid her smile of relief in the warm sweet cow smell, the fragrance of fresh milk foaming in a bucket. Maybe what he needed was to be stood on his ear once in a while.

So, Nora added the evening milking to her chores. And caring for the gray-and-white barred chickens, as well as the garden and the house.

One day, with the hay cut and cured, Carl wrestled the high racks for hauling hay onto the front and back of the wide wagon bed.

Nora wished for her brothers to come help him. Why didn't he share the haying work with some of his neighbors? The answer came to her immediately. He was too proud to ask for help. And, as Ingeborge had told her in the spring, Norwegians did not always take kindly to superior acting Germans. That Carl could act superior, she knew for a fact.

"Why do you care?" she asked herself one hot afternoon. She sank into the rocker with a jar of water in her hand. Some she sipped and some she dripped onto a cloth to cool her forehead—she had been hoeing the potatoes.

Down at the barn, Carl had parked the hay wagon under the four, cast-iron prongs that would lift the hay into the steadily filling hayloft. She could see his weariness in the slump of his shoulders. Climb up onto the hay wagon, set the forks, climb down, go around the barn, have the horses pull the rope that lifted the hay bundle up into the loft and back toward the pile. Trip the prongs and begin all over again. He needed some help.

Nora put Peder in the sling. A jug of water in her one hand, she took Kaaren's small grubby paw in the other. Down to the barn they strolled.

"Hi, Pa." Kaaren announced their presence.

Brownie lay panting under the wagon, his feathery tail fluffing the dirt. Kaaren crawled under with the dog and giggled when he licked her face.

"Here." Nora held out the cool water. Carl wiped his forehead and reached for the drink.

"Thank you." This time she understood his answer.

Carl chugged the drink and, when finished, wiped his mouth with the back of his hand.

"I will help you."

"You would do that?" Carl stared at her over the rim of the jar.

Nora nodded.

"Even after the way I've been acting?"

She nodded again. "Just tell me what you want me to do. I've driven horses before at home and I've also helped with gathering the hay." She tipped her head back, the better to study him from under the straw brim.

"But you have the baby."

She patted the sleeping form in her shawl slings. "He's fine. Peder likes being close, being carried like this."

"All right. But you'll tell me when . . . if. . . . " His gaze dropped to the sling and flicked back to her face.

"His name is Peder."

"I know." He sighed deeply. "When Peder needs you, he comes first." They heard a giggle from under the hay wagon and a smile flitted across Carl's face. "Would you please go around the barn and drive the team forward when I tell you to? I'll tell you when to stop, also."

Nora nodded. She leaned over and peered under the wagon. "Come, Kaaren."

Like Mary in the Scriptures, Nora pondered these things in her heart. For a Norwegian man to admit he had been wrong was like . . . like. . . .She could not think of anything to compare it with. And he had finally said his son's name—for the first time in nearly three months.

Thank You, Father. Thank You. Her heart sang.

Dusty, thirsty, and with sunburned cheeks, Nora waved as Carl left for the hayfield and his last load of hay. They would hoist it into the hayloft in the morning. Now, she just had the cows to milk and supper to fix. Peder whimpered and twisted in his sling—and a baby to feed, first of all. She turned and trudged up to the house.

"Nora. Nora." The call carried on the evening breeze.

Nora shaded her eyes, staring after the wagon. Carl stood on the front rack, waving his arm and yelling at her.

"What!"

"Leave the cows for me to milk."

She waved back in agreement. "Your pa is a good man," she said to Kaaren in particular and the world in general. The words sounded puny compared to the chorus in her heart.

Each Sunday, Nora felt tempted to beg Carl to take them to church but each time she remembered his anger at her Bible reading. How she would love to visit with Ingeborge. And hear the organ playing in church, Reverend Moen preaching in Norwegian, and people visiting after the service. On Sundays, she missed home and her family the most.

The first Sunday in August burned so hot even the birds hushed their singing. Nora spread a blanket out in the shade of the cottonwood trees. She sat propped against the tree trunk, her Bible in her lap, fanning herself, and singing to Kaaren. Peder lay beside her, entranced by the shifting leaf patterns.

Between songs, Nora eyed the western horizon, praying to see the mounds of black clouds that brought the cooling rain they so desperately needed. Hauling water to her garden used every bit of energy she could find. But, she reminded herself, Sunday was to be a day of rest, the good Lord said so Himself. She turned away from thoughts of Carl cultivating the corn.

When Kaaren's eyelids drooped, Nora took the most recent letter from Norway from her pocket and read the beloved words again. When she closed her eyes she could hear her mother saying the words she wrote. How far away Norway and the life there seemed now.

Her eyes must have been closed longer than she thought. She jerked awake. No, everything was the same. Kaaren slept, sprawled like a puppet with broken strings. Peder lay on his tummy, cheeks pink from the heat, his breath even and deep.

What bothered her?

She scanned the horizon again. A flat, black band separated the green prairie and the blue sky. Flat, not piled and puffed up like the life-giving clouds. She read her letter again. The black band grew wider.

Go to the house, an inner voice prompted.

"Don't be silly," Nora argued with herself. "The children are sleeping better than they have for days. It's cooler out here than anywhere else. There's nothing to fear."

The black band darkened, spreading now across the entire western horizon.

A grasshopper flew onto her skirt.

Nora brushed it off and bit her lip.

The band, no longer flat, undulated like a blanket settling onto a bed. A fat, green grasshopper crawled over Peder's back. Still asleep, Kaaren brushed one off her face. The action woke her. She sat up, whimpering and rubbing her eyes.

A sound like nothing Nora had ever heard seemed to come from the widening river of black.

A wave of fear brought Nora to her knees, scrambling to gather their belongings. "Kaaren, run to the house." She set the little girl on her feet and pushed her in the general direction.

"No-o-o." Kaaren wailed and wrapped her fist in Nora's skirt.

Nora clutched Peder to her chest with one arm. With the quilt flung over the other and the basket in her hand, she had no hand for the whining girl. She stared over her shoulder.

The apparition flowed nearer. The sound, like the buzzing of angry bees, filled her ears.

She looked down at her skirt. Three grasshoppers had landed there. She could feel another in her hair. Were they, too, afraid of the approaching menace?

"Kaaren, help me carry the basket." She bumped Kaaren's arm with the handle.

In spite of her blue eyes welling with tears, Kaaren obeyed. She grasped the basket with a chubby hand.

"Now!" Nora forced a smile on her face and a lilt in her voice. "Let's run."

In the past, she had dreamed of running and never getting to her destination. Now, it was so. With the baby bouncing in her arm and the basket thumping her thigh with every step, Nora felt like she was running through a quagmire. Instead of coming closer, the house seemed farther away every time she looked up.

After an eternity they collapsed on the porch. Kaaren held up her arm and giggled at a grasshopper with irridescent wings and bobbing feelers.

"See, Ma. Big bug." She poked him with her finger. Instead of hopping off, he flew away.

Nora looked from Kaaren to the porch posts. Bugs

had landed all over, their wings whirring and click-ing. They crawled onto her skirt, the quilt, and Kaaren's dress. She brushed several off Peder.

"Ugh." She looked up at the sky now dusky with flying insects. "Kaaren, brush them off and go in-side. Now!" Her tone allowed no chance of resist-ance. She brushed the marauding insects off the baby's things, her skirt, and apron. When the door closed behind them, she grabbed one from Kaaren's shoulder and threw it outside.

She laid Peder on his quilt on the floor and re-turned to stand at the screen door. Where was Carl? What was happening?

The cows bellowed from the pasture by the barn. As she watched, they stuck their tails straight in the air and the animals charged off across the pasture.

Should she go down and let them into the barn?

She looked out at her rosebush—its stalks writhed like living things. She bit her knuckles to keep from crying out. The bush was buried in gnawing, buzz-ing creatures.

Clouds of insects turned the day into dusk. Was the sun, too, being eaten alive by the invading hoard?

Her garden!

"Stay here!" She cracked the order and pointed to the quilt. Wide-eyed, Kaaren sat down by the baby. Nora grabbed another quilt off the bed and, clapping the straw hat onto her head, stormed out the door.

She ran to the garden, waving the quilt then, using it like a club, beat the bugs crawling over her plants. She shook it in the sky and screamed at the avenging hoard but they kept coming. The crunch of their feeding filled the air. They covered her hat, her arms, her face. She spit out the one that was crawling in her mouth.

Her arms ached from brandishing the quilt. "Fire. I'll burn them out."

She turned to the house. Kerosene, a torch of kerosene, would that work? How to get it burning? Would smoke drive them away? But what would she burn?

Hay! She ran to the barn with her tattered quilt in hand.

Slipping in with the door open only a crack, she spread the quilt on the floor and forked hay onto it. Then gathering up the corners, she half-carried, half-dragged it back to the garden. Her side ached; her legs quivered. She did not dare open her mouth to draw in the deep breaths she so desperately needed—the thought of swallowing a grasshopper made her gag.

She staggered to the house, grabbed a kerosene-filled lamp and the matches and dashed back outside again. "Stay there, Kaaren," she panted as she closed the door behind her.

She unscrewed the top of the lamp and poured the kerosene on the pile of hay. She scraped the match across the sole of her shoe and tossed the flaming bit of wood into the hay. The fuel caught; smoke rose in tendrils, then billowed up. Grasshoppers fell. But when the fire dimmed, the horde resumed as if nothing had happened.

Carl found her, kneeling in the dirt now bare of

the beans nearly ready to pick and the corn that had been starting to tassle. Rivulets of tears streaked across her skin darkened by smoke and dirt.

He picked her up and gathered her into his arms, brushing a kiss across her cheek.

Nora sobbed against the wall of his chest. "I . . . I tried so hard." She hiccuped between words. "N-nothing stopped them."

"I know. Shhhh, now." He murmured comfort but Nora was beyond hearing.

"I worked so hard and this flat land—it hates me. My garden gone—my family—no one." She thumped a shaking fist on his chest. "I want to laugh again—and dance—and see my friends. There's nothing left. Not-h-i-n-g."

"I know." Carl picked her up in his arms and carried her back to the house. He brushed the crawling insects off the porch steps and sat with her in his lap.

"Pa?" Kaaren stood inside the door, peeking through the screen.

"You be a good girl and stay there." Carl stroked the hair back from Nora's eyes and laid her head on his shoulder.

"But Ma's crying." Her voice quivered with tears.

"I know. Ma's sad." Carl continued to rock Nora in his arms. "Go see how Peder is."

"Pa, I want my ma-a-a."

Deep in her own fog, Nora heard the cry of her child. She sat up, only then realizing the comfort and strength of the arms that held her. She hiccuped again and wiped her eyes with the edge of her tattered and filthy apron.

Oh to be able to sink back and let herself float on that sea of calm that follows a cleansing cry. To stay wrapped up in arms so warm and safe. To listen again to the heart that thumped in perfect rhythm beneath her cheek. His two-day growth of beard scratched the tender skin of her cheek. How good it felt.

"M-a-a-a-a!"

Nora stood. When she swayed, Carl caught her around the waist. She looked up into his eyes so close and lost herself in their shimmering blue depths. With a sigh, she leaned her head against his chest again. This was home.

"M-a-a-a."

She could hear the rumble of Carl's answer to his daughter through his shirt. She took another deep breath and stepped back. "Let's go in. She needs us."

Still supported by his arm, they walked up the steps and opened the screen door.

Kaaren hurled herself at their legs.

Carl picked up his daughter and patted her back. Kaaren reached for Nora and wrapped her arms around them both.

"Big bug."

Nora looked up to see Kaaren picking a grasshopper from her father's hair.

"Here, Ma." Kaaren dropped it into Nora's hand and giggled when Nora made a face and threw the insect out the door.

After feeding Peder, Nora took a pan of tepid

water into the bedroom, closed the door, and took off her clothes. The water on her skin raised goosebumps but with each swipe of the cloth, she felt closer to being herself. When she had dried herself and changed into clean clothes, she bundled her dirty ones, tempted to stuff them into the stove and burn them.

She shook her head. All they needed was a good washing. She tied on a clean white apron and, picking up the pan of now black water, reentered the kitchen.

Carl too, had washed. Moisture darkened his sun-bleached hair to deep bronze. When he smiled, his teeth gleamed white against the tan of his lower face. That stubborn lock of hair half-covered the white line across his forehead left by his hat.

Her fingers itched to brush that lock of hair back into place. Instead, Nora emptied her pan of water into the sink and dipped new water into a pitcher. She unclasped her hair and leaning over the sink, poured the water over her scalp. With the last of the rose-scented soap she had brought with her from home, she washed her hair.

"Let me help." Carl removed the pitcher from her hand and poured the water over her hair to rinse it.

Nora twisted her head from side-to-side so all the soap could be rinsed away. How wonderful it felt to have someone help her like this. How wonderful to have Carl, stern Carl, rinse her hair. She felt a warmth pool in her middle and spread upward to her heart.

"Thank you." She wrung her hair out and with the

towel she had laid beside her, began drying her waist-length tresses.

"I . . . I think I'll go get started on the milking." Carl backed away. The urge to reach out and touch that rippling mass of gold caught him by surprise. He had only offered to help her. What was wrong with that?

As he brought in the cows, the questions remained in his mind. When he poured their feed, he stared at the flowing grain. Would there be anything left to harvest? What would he feed the livestock this winter? While he had had a good hay crop, hay alone was not enough. The pigs and chickens could not live on hay.

He thought back. The flood of Nora's tears weighed him down until he felt like his shoulders dragged on the floor. Was she really so unhappy here? She had never said so. But why would she? When had he encouraged her to talk with him, other than to learn English?

He picked up his stool and started on the second cow. One bad thing about milking, it gave you too much time to think.

When he had finished and let the cows out again, one resolve shone clear. He had promised to send her back to Norway and that he would do.

He picked up the brimming pails. But, if he paid for her ticket, how could he hire a housekeeper? Where would he find the money to buy grain for his cows, food for his household?

He knew what life was like after the grasshoppers came. They ate everything in sight. Only those vegetables below the surface were saved.

But his potato field was not mature enough to have set potatoes yet.

"God, help me, I don't know what to do." Carl did not realize he had uttered a prayer. He poured the milk into the skimming pans in the cool well house, keeping half a pail out for the house.

He stopped with one foot on the porch steps and looked up at the heavens. Stars peeked out through their windows in the black velvet of the sky. A breeze rattled the bare branches of the cottonwood trees.

He listened carefully. The whirr and crunch of the invading horde was no more.

He walked into the kitchen and set the milk bucket in the sink. "I'll go into town tomorrow and telegraph reservations to New York for your ticket back to Norway."

twelve

"But I don't want to go," Nora said.

"I will live up to my word," Carl answered. "When we married I promised you could return to Norway."

Nora could feel her mind running like a crazed thing caught in a maze. "B-but, you have no housekeeper for my . . . the children."

"I will work something out." He turned from her and went to stand at the window.

God, Father God. Please help me. Why does he bring this up now? The prayer continued as she dished the baked beans onto their plates.

The ticking of the clock was the only sound in the silence. She had hurried to put the children to bed. And now she wished they were here to need her. Didn't Carl need her? Who else would love his children, his house, and, yes—his entire farm—like she did? Who would love such a contrary person as him like she did?

She nearly dropped the plate of molasses-laden beans. *When had love come into her heart?*

"Your supper is ready," she called as he stood looking out at the blackness.

Carl sighed as he sat down. He studied the food on the plate before him.

Nora watched him. "Do you want something else?" She jumped up. "I forgot the bread." Returning to the table, she set down a plate of sliced bread and slipped back into her chair. She cast around in her mind for something to say to break the silence.

"The cows . . . they are all right?"

Carl nodded. He scooped a fork of beans and ate them.

"They will still give milk?"

He nodded again. "The grasshoppers didn't bother them, just ate all their feed. Thank God I got the hay in before this happened."

Yes. You must thank God, Nora thought. *When you can thank Him again all will be right with you.* She forced herself to eat. Put the beans on your fork . . . chew and swallow. A bite of bread . . . chew and swallow. Swallowing was the hard part. The boulder, lodged in her throat, made it difficult.

"We'll know more in the daylight. Sometimes, they skip whole fields. I've seen times when one farm would be wiped out and the next one not touched." Carl nodded and finally looked at her, really looked at her. "We'll know more in the morning."

"Please God, let there be something left," Nora prayed on her knees that night. "I am so confused. I did want to go back to Norway. Now, I want to stay here. How do I explain this to him?" She closed her eyes and let the breeze from the window cool her cheeks. One tear slipped from between her eyelids and trickled down her cheek. "Your will, Father. Amen."

Early the next morning, Nora walked to the edge

of her garden. She wrapped her arms around her middle and squeezed against the pain that ripped through her. The sun, shining on what used to be her thriving garden, showed not one blade or leaf of green. The black dirt looked like no one had ever planted there. Gray ashes lay where she had tried to burn the marauders out.

The trees, as if caught in the nakedness of winter, raised empty fingers to the sky. The fields lay bare, like her garden.

As she staggered back to the porch, dead bodies of the winged creatures crunched beneath her feet. She sank down onto the steps, the weight of the destruction too heavy to bear.

By her knee, one tough cane was all that remained of her rosebush. Nora reached down with a shaking finger and stroked the stalk, stripped even of thorns. *I never picked one of your blossoms. The third one had just opened. I was waiting for more. So many buds . . . now all are gone.* She buried her face in her knees and let loose the sobs that cramped her chest.

By the time Carl returned from the morning milking, her nose still dripped and her eyes were red. She wiped her nose with a handkerchief and tucked it back into her pocket.

"Breakfast will be ready as soon as you are." When she tried to smile, her lower lip quivered.

"Where's Kaaren and Peder?" Carl glanced around the kitchen.

"Still sleeping. Yesterday must have worn them out."

"Me, too." He poured sour cream over his pancakes and added a spoonful of jam on top. After only one bite, he put his fork down. "I rode out to the fields at dawn. There's nothing left." The words dropped into the silent kitchen and spread like ripples on a smooth lake.

Nora closed her eyes. "What will you do?"

"I'll have to buy grain both for feed and for seed next spring."

She waited for him to continue.

Outside on the porch, Brownie scratched at a flea, his leg thumping against the boards.

Carl shook his head. His voice seemed distant, far away like he was talking to someone else. "With no harvest, my savings will go to pay the farm payments. Or, I'll see about another loan." Teeth clenched, he growled. "I hate to borrow money, to be beholding—to anyone."

Silence took over the farm again. One day on a return trip from town, Carl tossed a letter on the table. He shook his head. "Too late."

"What do you mean?" Nora turned from kneading the bread dough.

"A letter from a woman who would like the job of housekeeper. She can even speak English." He poured himself a cup of coffee. "Your reservation is scheduled for the first of October."

Her breath escaped in a hiss, as if someone had punched her in the belly.

Carl tipped back his head and drained the coffee cup. "I heard about a farm that needs hands for the harvest. Can you manage here, if I'm gone a few days?"

"Yah." She took in a deep breath, one that stiffened her backbone. It was now or never.

"Carl, I want to talk to you." Nora formed the dough into a smooth mound and placed it back into the earthenware bowl to rise. As her fingers performed their usual functions, her mind cast around for the right words.

He started to walk out the door.

"Carl! Sit down." She pointed at the chair. Appalled at her tone, she added a gentle, "Please."

He sat. Back straight as a poker, face about as unbending, he turned to face her. A muscle jumped in his cheek.

Nora swallowed. Why had she said anything? She wound her fingers in her apron.

"I told you I don't want to go back to Norway."

Carl waved his fingers, like brushing off a bug. His look branded her a silly female who does not know her own mind.

"We agreed."

"I know. But . . . but things have changed. You don't have money to spare for my ticket. Peder and Kaaren . . . they . . . they need me." Her heart wanted to cry, and *I care about you,* but, instead, she sat straighter and forced her errant heart to remain still.

"You want me to go back on my word?" Blue eyes drilled ice chips into hers.

"No, no." She shook her head. "You wouldn't be if it is me that changed my mind."

Carl shook his head. "You are so young. How can you know your mind? What is best for you?" He pushed himself to his feet, the matter closed. "I may be gone for as long as a week. You'll have the team in case you need them."

Nora stood at the doorway to watch him swing himself up onto the bare back of the bay gelding. He picked up his sack that he had rested on a fence post, touched a finger to the black hat brim, and turned the horse to trot down the lane.

Tears, pooling in her eyes, made him shimmer and fade in the bright sunlight.

"Where is Pa?" Kaaren asked at the table before eating her mush.

"Gone." Uttering the one word took much of Nora's strength.

Kaaren raised her gaze from her meal to Nora's face. Her bottom lip quivered and tears flooded her eyes. "Pa gone like my Ma?" The question ended on a whimper.

"Oh, no, Kaaren. Your pa just went to help another farmer with a harvest. He'll come back soon, very soon."

Every morning, every noon, and again at bedtime, Kaaren posed the question. "Pa's coming now?"

"Soon, little one, soon." Nora hugged and petted both children, tickling Kaaren to make her giggle and tossing Peder in the air to hear his belly laugh. With no garden to care for, she concentrated all her care on the children and the livestock.

She sewed Kaaren two new dresses out of some material she had found tucked away in a drawer. She altered a cotton dress of Anna's that hung in a closet so she would have something cooler to wear. The blue print fabric was on the table, waiting for her to begin cutting.

"You're going to need clothes, too, one of these days," she told Peder one afternoon. He waved chubby fists like he knew exactly what she was saying and agreed wholeheartedly. They must have saved Kaaren's baby things, she thought while holding the bottle for Peder. But where?

She searched the house over and finally looked up the stairs. She had only been up there to change the sheets on Carl's bed. With one hand on the rail, she mounted the stairs. Heat, like when she opened her oven door, met her when she opened the door to his room. It was as orderly as his barn. Clothes hung on hooks, good boots were polished and lined up under the black wool suit he had worn the day of the funeral.

She heard Kaaren calling from outside. Leaning over the table in front of the window, she pushed up the sash and stuck her head out.

"I'm up here. Upstairs. What is it?"

Kaaren came running around the corner of the house. "Hi, Ma." She stopped, legs spread apart, and, leaning back to get a good view, waved. Her giggle floated on the still air. "Read now?"

Nora shook her head. "Soon." She drew back in, careful not to bang her head. A piece of paper drifted off the table so she leaned over to pick it up.

Carl's careful lettering, so familiar to her after the long English lessons, caught her eye. She read, the words leaping off the page and branding her heart.

> *Dear Adolph,*
> *I am writing to ask if you and Viola would take*

> *care of my children for me. If you could come*
> *for them after harvest since I have no one here*
> *to feed my animals if I leave. The grasshop-*
> *pers ate. . . .*

The words blurred. How could he?

Baby clothes forgotten, Nora put the paper back onto the table and staggered down the stairs. He really meant to send her back to Norway. What she wanted did not matter. All that counted was his word.

She slumped into the rocker. He did not care for her then, not at all. To him, she was just the house-keeper he had had to marry to save their reputations. "Dear God, what do I do now? I thought he was coming to care for me. But, I was wrong." The heaviness sat on her both inside and out.

The days and nights were so hot their clothes stuck to their bodies. Peder whimpered from a prickly heat rash and even Kaaren drooped like a flower that needs a drink.

The week stretched into ten days. Would Carl never come home?

But when he did ride up on the bay horse, nothing changed. Except now, Nora did not have the animals to care for and, with more time on her hands, she had too many hours to think. She tried to remember the good times with her family, to remind herself that she would be seeing them soon, to think about wading in the stream that rushed and tumbled over the rocks on its way to the Norwegian sea. Cool water. Laughter—and love again.

"Would you please milk the cows in the morning?" Carl asked one evening. "I'm driving over to the creek bed north of here to cut fence posts. I'll be home before dinner so I can take the butter and cream into town."

Nora looked at him, amazement dropping her jaw. He had not strung so many words together at one time since . . . since the grasshoppers.

"Yah, I can do that."

In the morning, Nora went about her chores with a lighter step. Did Carl's request mean that he was drawing out of his silence? Or that they would go back to talking in the evening?

But dinner time came and Carl did not appear. Nora pushed the pan of fried chicken off to the side of the stove, along with the gravy and the last of the tiny potatoes she had dug up after the hoppers ate the plants.

She walked around the outside of the house and, shading her eyes, searched the northern horizon. Nothing. At the one o'clock vigil, she saw a hawk floating on the rising air currents. At two, a snake of fear slithered around her middle—Carl never broke his word—something had happened.

Nora ran down to the barn and, after grabbing a bridle off the wall and can of oats from the nearly empty feed bin, slipped through the gate rails and into the pasture. "Here, boy." She shook the can, calling the new horse. The cows mooed in response. At the sound of rattling oats, the dark bay horse raised his head and trotted toward her.

"Good boy, good." Nora fed him the grain from

her palm and slipped the reins around his neck. Holding the reins securely with one hand, she slid the bit between his teeth and the headstall over his ears. "What a good horse," she murmured soothing words, all the while buckling the straps in place and leading him up to the fence.

At the house, she tied his reins to the fence and dashed inside. "Kaaren, bring me Peder's shawl. We're going to find your pa."

How would she mount? By herself it was not a problem. She had learned early how to leap on a horse. But, what about with Peder and Kaaren. "Father, help me." She took a deep breath and exhaled, letting her shoulders drop and the tension leave. The porch. Surely, the rail was high enough for her to slide onto this animal's back and grab Kaaren the same way.

She led the horse up to the porch, grateful for his docile manner. Someone had trained him well. With Peder's sling locked over one shoulder, she mounted the railing and slung her leg over the horse's back. Her skirts bunched up around her knees but she and Peder were secure.

"Kaaren, climb up on the rail, just like I did." Kaaren stuck a finger in her mouth and hung back.

Nora gritted her teeth. "We'll go find Pa. Good horse." She patted the bay's neck. "See? Climb up now."

Kaaren did like she was told.

Nora leaned over and, with one arm, grabbed the little girl around her waist. With the other, she settled Kaaren's legs across the horse and firmly against her chest.

"Thank You, God. Thank You." Nora dropped a kiss on Kaaren's hair. "Such a good girl. Now, hang on tight to this." She made Kaaren's hands grab onto the horse's mane. "Now, let's go find Pa."

Nora reined the horse around and out of the yard. Once on the prairie, she nudged him to a trot. With the hand that held the reins and guided the horse also anchoring Kaaren, Nora tried with the other hand to keep Peder from bouncing out of his sling. To her surprise, the rough ride did not bother the baby at all.

"Faster, Ma." Kaaren giggled and swung her legs, her hands gripping the coarse black mane.

Nora wanted to kick the animal into a lope but the thought of all of them being dumped onto the ground made her more cautious. As they settled into the pace, the horse's heavy feet thudded across the soil stripped bare by the grasshoppers. New blades of green promised the return of life.

Ahead, Nora could see the tops of denuded willow trees that lined the creek. What should be a spot of green on the horizon stood pale as the rest of the earth.

Where could he be? The creek curved and rambled for many miles. Her questions kept time with her prayers.

"Carl!" The bouncing gait of the horse kept her voice from carrying like it should. She reined him to a stop and, with both hands bracketing her mouth, called again.

A horse whinnied off to their left.

Nora nudged the bay to a trot again. Ears pricked, he lifted his head and whinnied back at a sound he alone could hear.

Looking ahead, Nora spotted the wagon tracks she had been searching for all along. They led over a hump and down into the flat area bordering the creek.

The horse whinnied again, much closer this time. Nora gave her horse his head and he saw the team before she did. His whinny sounded even louder than back up on the plain.

The team stood patiently, still harnessed to the wagon. The larger gray horse snorted and tossed his head. A few fence posts were in the wagon bed.

But where was Carl?

"Hush." Nora placed her fingers over Kaaren's mouth and strained to hear any noise. Harnesses jingled; horses snorted; a crow cawed his announcement that someone new had entered his territory.

"Carl!" Her voice cracked as she gave his name two syllables. "Ca-rl!"

"Yes."

Had she really heard a sound? The horses pricked their ears in the same direction. She called again.

This time the response came stronger.

She nudged her horse forward, skirting the wagon and angling up the creek bed.

"Carl!" This time she knew she was on the right track. She pushed through the willow thicket, protecting their faces with her bent arms.

He lay on the ground, next to a fallen tree. Even from this distance, she could see his blood-soaked leg.

thirteen

"Go get the wagon!" he cried.

Nora struggled between the desire to leap down and make sure he was not bleeding to death and the knowledge that what he ordered was imperative—she had to get the wagon. She turned her horse around and headed back the way they had come.

The patient team pricked their ears and whinnied as soon as they saw the bay.

"Kaaren, I'm going to let you down into the wagon so be ready." Nora nudged the horse right next to the rear of the wagon. "Here we go. Now, slide your leg over his neck, that's right." She spoke in a gentle voice, calm and patient but inside she was screaming—*hurry! Hurry!* "Good. Now hang onto my hand and just slide down."

Kaaren landed on the board floor with a thump. "See, Ma." She grinned up at Nora.

"Yah, good." Nora clutched Peder in his sling with one hand while she leaned forward and swung one leg behind her. Together, they slid to the ground, as if they had been dismounting like this all their lives. She quickly tied the bay's reins to the rear of the wagon and ran to untie the team. Still bearing her heavy burden, she climbed up onto the seat and released the brake.

"Kaaren, come up here and sit down." She pointed to a spot right behind her, still in the wagon bed. As

Kaaren, eyes big, stumbled over the posts, Nora settled Peder in her lap.

He squirmed and let out a yowl, clearly unhappy with such rough treatment.

"Good girl." Nora threw a smile over her shoulder and slapped the reins. "Hup now, boys." The team jerked the wagon to a start.

Nora eyed the thicket ahead. No time to find a way around it. "Hang on, Kaaren." She sheltered Peder with her body and forced the team into and through the slapping, tearing branches. She stopped the wagon within inches of Carl.

He lay on the ground, eyes closed, his face chalky white as if all the blood had drained from his body.

"Oh, God, dear God." Her words ran into a litany, Nora not even aware that she was talking out loud. She lifted Peder in his sling over her head and twisted around to lay him beside Kaaren.

"Take care of baby now." She nodded and smiled at the little girl like this was some new game. "I'll get your pa for you." Nora jumped to the ground and knelt by Carl's inert body.

"You came," he said. "I prayed you'd come."

She could hardly hear his voice, weak as it was. "Yah, my love, we are here. Now you must help me."

"Don't . . . worry about . . . bandage."

She bent closer to hear him.

"Used belt . . . for tourniquet . . . stop bleeding."

"Yes, Carl. Now, I'm going to pull you up to a sitting position." She wrapped one arm around his back and grasped his closer arm with her hand.

"Now!" She pulled, he pushed.

He bit his lip against the groan.

"Now, put your arm over my shoulders and, together, we lift."

This time, he could not suppress the groan.

Nora clamped her teeth together. Sweat popped out on her brow from the strain. But, they were standing.

"Lean on me." This time it was she who groaned as his weight shifted onto her.

Together they took the two steps needed for him to collapse into the bed of the wagon. He pulled himself forward with his arms until his legs were in the wagon, too.

"Pa!" Kaaren had watched all the goings-on with huge eyes. Now, the tears poured out and she threw herself against his chest.

Nora climbed up into the wagon bed. After making sure Carl was secure, she hefted the squalling Peder in his sling and hauled it back over her head and shoulder. Then, she climbed over the back of the seat, sat down, and slapped the team into motion.

The ride to town lasted an eternity of dust, crying children, jouncing, tears, and Carl's fading in and out. When she finally drove down the main street of Soldall, she had no idea how to find Doctor Harmon. For what seemed like the past 400 miles, she had been praying he would just be there.

"Can you tell me where Doctor Harmon lives?" she yelled to the first person she saw.

The man trotted up to the wagon and peered in. "Oh, heaven. Here, I'll show you." He leaped onto the seat. "Turn right, there, by the blacksmith." He pointed ahead of them. "What happened to him?" He spoke softly so Carl would not hear.

Nora was not sure if Carl was conscious or not. He had not said anything for the last—forever. "He was out at the creek, cutting fence posts. The ax slipped."

"Turn left, here. That's Doc's house and office with the light in the window. I'll help carry your man in." He leaped to the ground before the team came to a full halt. "Harmon!" His yell could be heard clear to Fargo.

A graying man in his shirt sleeves threw open the door. "What'd ya need?"

"Something to carry this man in on. Leg's cut bad."

While the doctor pulled his head back in, Nora climbed back over the seat and laid Peder on the wagon floor. "You care for Peder." She took Kaaren by the hand and sat her beside the baby.

She knelt by Carl's head and put her hand on his chest. Yes, he was still breathing. *Oh, dear Lord. If we've ever needed You, we need You, now.*

"All right, ma'am, we'll take him now." Doctor Harmon slid the poles of a stretcher in beside his patient. "Carl!" He turned to look at Nora. "What did he do?"

All the while he was talking, he and the other man lifted Carl onto the stretcher, slid it to the rear of the wagon, and, with one man at each end, lifted the heavy burden. Together, they carried their load up the steps and into the doctor's office.

Nora climbed down and, grabbing Kaaren and Peder, followed the stretcher carriers. She stood in the doorway as they lifted Carl onto a flat, well-padded wooden table.

"Pa, Pa." Kaaren sniffled and cried, hiding her face in Nora's filthy skirt. Peder, worn out from all the crying, only whimpered now and then.

"Will he . . . can you . . . ?" The words stuck in Nora's throat. She wanted to throw herself across Carl's chest and howl out her terror, her love, her prayers. She lifted Peder higher in her arms and buried her face in his sling.

"He's alive." Doctor Harmon looked up only long enough to make eye contact with her. "That's all I can say right now."

"Now, dear." A woman's voice came from behind her. "I'm Mrs. Harmon. Why don't you come with me for now. There's nothing you can do here. The doctor will do the best he can."

Nora turned. Lifting her feet to follow the roundly padded woman with the kind voice took all her strength.

"Let me get you a cup of coffee and maybe your little girl would like a glass of milk and a cookie?"

Nora pulled herself back to the moment. "Please, show me the way to Reverend Moen's. Ingeborge will care for my . . . for Kaaren and Peder. Then, I will come back."

"If that is what you want. But you are welcome to stay here."

"Thank you."

Mrs. Harmon gave instructions while she walked Nora back out to the wagon. She handed Kaaren to her after Nora had climbed up to the seat. "I'll see you in a while then?"

Nora nodded. "Thank you." She flicked the reins and the horses broke into a trot.

With a small town like Soldall, the directions were not too complex and she found the parsonage without any trouble. Light beamed from the windows on the ground floor, welcoming her back.

Nora slumped against the board that formed the seat back. Now that Carl was someone else's responsibility, she felt limp, drained of every thread of strength and will. She could feel tears rolling down her cheeks. When had she begun to cry? When had she not been crying?

She stared at the walk from the fence and up the steps to the front door. Could she make it? Would her knees support her?

"God, please." She leaned forward and wrapped the reins around the pole. "You can climb down by yourself, Kaaren. Mary lives here." She pulled herself to her feet. With Peder in one arm, she used the other to brace herself and swung her leg over the wagon side. She stumbled as she landed and the jerk made Peder cry again.

The door opened. Light poured down the walk. "Is anyone—oh no," Reverend Moen's voice deepened. "Nora, what has happened to you? Ingeborge, come quick." As he spoke, he leaped from the steps and wrapped his arm around Nora's shoulders. Ingeborge appeared before her and lifted the whimpering Peder in his sling over Nora's head.

Nora swayed from the lightness of releasing one of her burdens but John steadied her. They led her inside and sat her in the rocking chair.

"Now, tell me. What has happened?" Ingeborge placed a cup of coffee in Nora's hands and closed the trembling fingers around the warmth. "Drink first."

"Peder. He hasn't been fed for hours."

"Mary, please fix a bottle. John, could you please take the mite in and change him?"

Nora could feel Kaaren attached to her knee.

"Pa's hurt. His leg is bleeding, bad."

"He cut himself with an ax cutting down fence posts in the creek bottom. We brought him to Doctor Harmon's." Nora raised her gaze to encounter the sympathy flowing from the face of her friend. "Oh, Ingeborge, he might die. So much blood lost."

"Drink your coffee. John will take you back over there as soon as you have the strength. The children will be just fine here, with us."

Her soothing voice and loving hands brought a measure of peace back to Nora. And with it, the strength to pull herself to her feet.

"Mange takk." Nora then went back to the doctor's house and Reverend Moen went with her.

"The doctor is still working with him," Mrs. Harmon said when she met Reverend Moen and Nora at the door. "Why don't you come right in here and have a seat?"

Nora followed her into the parlor and sat down on the chair nearest the door.

"I'll get you each a cup of coffee." Mrs. Harmon bustled out.

"If you don't mind," Reverend Moen leaned over her. "I pray best on my feet and pacing. Will that bother you?"

Nora shook her head. "We need all the prayers we can get."

Several cups of coffee later, Doctor Harmon entered the room. "I've done what I can and I'm sorry to tell you, it don't look good. He's lost a lotta blood. All's I can say, is he's in the good Lord's hands now."

"Can I see him?" asked Nora.

"If'n ya want. He's unconscious. Won't know you're there."

"No matter. I want to be with him."

"Just remember, he looks bad." He looked her over. " 'Pears to me you don't look so good yerself. I have an idea. You spend some time with that man of yours and Mrs. Harmon'll heat some water so's you can get cleaned up." He opened the door to a room with a bed. "Here he is."

Nora looked at the white face on the pillow. She stumbled, clamping her teeth against the whirling in her head.

"Grab her." She heard the voice from a great distance.

Arms helped her into a chair and a hand forced her head between her knees. "Easy, now. Just stay that way until the spell passes."

Nora took a deep breath. Her head cleared. Her stomach retreated back to its rightful position.

When she raised her head, she picked up Carl's hand that lay on top of the blankets. She studied his face, every dear line, all the while stroking his hand.

"If we can keep the infection from setting in, every hour he makes it is for the best."

"I'm not leaving him."

"Didn't think you would."

Nora followed Mrs. Harmon's instructions. Get

cleaned up, eat, drink, go back to Carl. There was never any change but she felt needed there.

"We have to keep him drinking so spoon water into his mouth every fifteen minutes or so." The doctor showed her how. With panic trapped in her throat, she watched until she saw Carl swallow. "That's good." Doctor Harmon left her with a spoon and pitcher of water.

Grateful for something to do, Nora followed orders. Somewhere in the wee hours, loving hands covered her with a light blanket. Every time she nodded off, she would wake on the minute to administer the water. With every spoonful, she reminded Carl that she loved him, her words soft and gentle.

People came and went through the next day. At one point, Doctor Harmon sent Nora off to bed where she slept for several hours before appearing at the door again to resume her post.

In the early morning, Nora had heard the clock strike three o'clock. She jerked fully awake. What was different? Carl? She clasped his hand. Ears straining, she listened to his breathing. Was it slower? Did it hesitate?

"Carl!"

She listened again. A breath . . . a pause . . . a breath. Each slower and fainter.

"Carl! You hear me? Listen to me! You can't die. We need you here. I love you, Carl Detschman!" She gripped his hand. "Don't you die on me!"

She held her breath. *Carl, breathe. God, please, make him breathe.*

She waited. The moment stretched to eternity—

and back.

Carl took a breath and let it out. And another. And another.

Nora wept.

An hour later, when the doctor came to relieve her, he nodded as she told her story. "Right about this time, the body is at its lowest. Lose patients mostly right about now." He clasped Carl's wrist between his thumb and forefinger. "Pulse is stronger." He applied the stethoscope to the man's chest. "Breathing better, too. I'd say he's passed the crisis." He stood straight again. "Will you go to bed now?"

Nora shook her head.

"Thought not. Just remember, I don't want to be doctoring you, too."

About noon, Carl regained consciousness. Nora watched his eyelids flutter. She placed the back of her fingers against his cheek. His eyelids fluttered again and this time he looked at her.

"Ah, Nora, love." A whisper so faint that if she had not been bending close, she might have missed it. His eyes closed again. One corner of his mouth tipped up ever so slightly.

After that, each time he woke he was stronger. Each time he called her "love."

The next day, he raised a hand to stroke her cheek, to brush away an errant tear. "Crying?"

"Tears of joy." She turned her face and kissed the palm of his hand.

That afternoon, Carl drank the good beef broth that Nora spooned into his mouth. When they were finished, he smiled at her. "I have something to tell you."

"Yah?" She leaned on her elbows beside him on the bed.

"When I was so sick?"

She nodded.

"One time, there was a long black tunnel." He paused. "I was going through it to reach a light at the other end. I couldn't wait to get to the light. It kept calling me but then I heard your voice. I finally reached the light, so . . . so peaceful." He paused again.

Nora watched his face. It glowed like candles were lit inside.

"I wanted to keep on going . . . the love there. Perfect love."

The wonder in his voice, the joy on his face. Nora could feel tears running down her cheeks again.

"But you called to me. You said not to die. You said you loved me."

The touch of his hand on hers, the touch of angel wings.

He smiled. "So I came back." His eyes fluttered closed and he slept.

"Nora?"

She sat up, sleep falling away like the dropping of a stone. Night still darkened the window. "Yah?"

"Will you marry me?"

"We *are* married. Don't you remember?" She smoothed that stubborn lock of hair off his forehead.

"No, I mean a real wedding—in the church. When I was lying there by the creek, I kept praying you would come. I begged God to let me live. A man comes face-to-face with what he's done wrong at a time like that. And you came."

"You said you'd be back for dinner. You always keep your word." She grinned, a teasing grin that made him smile back. "So, I went to see what kept you from your word."

"So, will you?"

"Will I what?"

"Marry me—again?"

"Can we wait until my sister Clara arrives? She should be here any day now."

"We can wait. I want to stand before Reverend Moen on my own two feet."

"And in the church."

"In the church." He wrinkled his brow. "How is Clara coming?"

"Someone sent her a ticket."

"Who?"

Nora shrugged. "I don't know. We'll ask her when she gets here."

Silence reigned in the sick room. Carl raised her hand and brought it to his lips. "I broke my word."

"Oh?"

"You won't be going back to Norway."

Nora chuckled. "I tried to tell you that, but you are so stubborn." She laid her head on his chest. "Will our children be bullheaded, like their pa?"

He chuckled into her hair. "Look, my Nora. Out the window."

Feather clouds glowed pink and silver as the returning sun promised a new Dakota dawn for Carl and Nora.

A Letter To Our Readers

Dear Reader:

In order that we might better contribute to your reading enjoyment, we would appreciate your taking a few minutes to respond to the following questions and return to:

> Karen Carroll, Editor
> Heartsong Presents
> P.O. Box 719
> Uhrichsville, Ohio 44683

1. Did you enjoy reading *Dakota Dawn*?
   - ☐ Very much. I would like to see more books by this author!
   - ☐ Moderately
   - ☐ I would have enjoyed it more if

   _____

2. Where did you purchase this book?_____

   _____

3. What influenced your decision to purchase this book?
   - ☐ Cover   ☐ Back cover copy
   - ☐ Title   ☐ Friends
   - ☐ Publicity   ☐ Other _____

4. Please rate the following elements from 1 (poor) to 10 (superior).
   - ❑ Heroine
   - ❑ Hero
   - ❑ Setting
   - ❑ Plot
   - ❑ Inspirational theme
   - ❑ Secondary characters

5. What settings would you like to see in Heartsong Presents Books?

   _____

   _____

6. What are some inspirational themes you would like to see treated in future books?

   _____

   _____

7. Would you be interested in reading other Heartsong Presents Books?
   - ❑ Very interested
   - ❑ Moderately interested
   - ❑ Not interested

8. Please indicate your age range:
   - ❑ Under 18
   - ❑ 18-24
   - ❑ 25-34
   - ❑ 35-45
   - ❑ 46-55
   - ❑ Over 55

Name _____

Occupation _____

Address _____

City_____ State _____ Zip _____

The "Miranda Trilogy"
by Grace Livingston Hill

The "Miranda Trilogy" delightfully follows the lives of three different women whose lives are inextricably intertwined.

These beautiful hardback volumes, published at $9.95 each, are available through Heartsong Presents at $4.97 each. Buy all three at $13.95 and save even more!

_____ **GLH1 MARCIA SCHUYLER**—When her older sister Kate runs off with another man on the eve of her wedding, Marcia Schuyler marries Kate's heartbroken beau and strives for a happy marriage.

_____**GLH2 PHOEBE DEAN**—A brief encounter with a handsome stranger brings romance and hope to a lovely girl who is being courted by a cruel widower.

_____**GLH3 MIRANDA**—Raised by her stern and uncaring grandparents, spunky Miranda finds a real home with David and Marcia Spafford as their housekeeper. Deep within Miranda's thoughts is her abiding love for Allan Whitney, accused murderer and town black sheep, who fled with Miranda's help twelve years earlier.

Great New Inspirational Fiction

from HEARTS♥NG PRESENTS

Biblical Novel Collection #1
by Lee Webber

<u>*Two complete inspirational novels in one volume.*</u>

_____ BNC1 **CALL ME SARAH**—Can Sarah, like Queen Esther
be used by God . . . even as a slave in Herod's place?
CAPERNAUM CENTURION—One Centurion's
life is irrevocably changed by his encounter with a
certain Nazarene.

Citrus County Mystery Collection #1

by Mary Carpenter Reid

<u>Two complete inspirational mystery and romance novels in one volume.</u>

_____ CCM1 **TOPATOPA**—Can Alyson Kendricks make an historic
village come alive . . . without becoming history herself?
DRESSED FOR DANGER—Roxanne Shelton's
fashion designs were the key to her success . . . but
did they unlock a closet of secrets?

*BOTH COLLECTIONS ARE AVAILABLE FOR $3.97 EACH THROUGH
HEARTSONG PRESENTS. ORIGINALLY PUBLISHED AT $7.95 EACH.*

LOVE A GREAT LOVE STORY?

Introducing Heartsong Presents —
Your Inspirational Book Club

Heartsong Presents Christian romance reader's service will provide you with four never before published romance titles every month! In fact, your books will be mailed to you at the same time advance copies are sent to book reviewers. You'll preview each of these new and unabridged books before they are released to the general public.

These books are filled with the kind of stories you have been longing for—stories of courtship, chivalry, honor, and virtue. Strong characters and riveting plot lines will make you want to read on and on. Romance is not dead, and each of these romantic tales will remind you that Christian faith is still the vital ingredient in an intimate relationship filled with true love and honest devotion.

Sign up today to receive your first set. Send no money now. We'll bill you only $9.97 post-paid with your shipment. Then every month you'll automatically receive the latest four "hot off the press" titles for the same low post-paid price of $9.97. That's a savings of 50% off the $4.95 cover price. When you consider the exaggerated shipping charges of other book clubs, your savings are even greater!

THERE IS NO RISK—you may cancel at any time without obligation. And if you aren't completely satisfied with any selection, return it for an immediate refund.

TO JOIN, just complete the coupon below, mail it today, and get ready for hours of wholesome entertainment.

Now you can curl up, relax, and enjoy some great reading full of the warmhearted spirit of romance.